S N O W   A N G E L S

SNOW ANGELS

STEWART O'NAN

DOUBLEDAY

New York London Toronto Sydney Auckland

PUBLISHED BY DOUBLEDAY
a division of
Bantam Doubleday Dell Publishing Group, Inc.
1540 Broadway, New York, New York 10036

DOUBLEDAY and the portrayal of an anchor
with a dolphin are trademarks of Doubleday,
a division of Bantam Doubleday Dell Publishing Group, Inc.

Excerpt from *One Fish, Two Fish, Red Fish, Blue Fish* by Dr. Seuss. TM
and copyright © 1960 and renewed 1988 by Dr. Seuss Enterprises,
L.P. Reprinted by permission of Random House, Inc.
Excerpt from "Returning" from *For the Union Dead* by Robert
Lowell. Copyright © 1964 by Robert Lowell and copyright renewed
© 1992 by Harriet Lowell, Sheridan Lowell and Caroline Lowell.
Reprinted by permission of Farrar, Straus & Giroux, Inc.

Book design by Jennifer Ann Daddio

The author gratefully acknowledges the support of the Pirate's Alley
William Faulkner Society, with special thanks to Joe DeSalvo and
Rosemary James, and to my generous benefactress,
Mrs. Adelaide Wisdom Benjamin.

Library of Congress Cataloging-in-Publication Data
O'Nan, Stewart, 1961–
Snow angels : a novel / Stewart O'Nan. — 1st ed.
p.   cm.
I. Title.
PS3565.N316S65   1994
813'.54—dc20   94-12037
CIP

ISBN 0-385-47574-8

3   5   7   9   10   8   6   4   2

For my mother and father and John

Nothing is deader than this small town main street,
where the venerable elm sickens, and hardens
with tarred cement, where no leaf
is born, or falls, or resists till winter.

But I remember its former fertility,
how everything came out clearly
in the hour of credulity
and young summer, when this street
was already somewhat overshaded,
and here at the altar of surrender,
I met you,
the death of thirst in my brief flesh.

ROBERT LOWELL

S N O W A N G E L S

O N E

I WAS IN THE BAND the fall my father left, in the second
row of trombones, in the middle because I was a fresh-
man. Tuesdays and Wednesdays after school we practiced in the music room, but on Fridays Mr.
Chervenick led us outside in our down jackets and

tasseled Steeler hats and shitkicker boots and across the footbridge that spanned the interstate to the middle school soccer field, where, like the football team itself, we ran square-outs and curls and a maneuver Mr. Chervenick called an oblique, with which, for the finale of every halftime show, we described—all 122 of us—a whirling funnel approximating our school's nickname, the Golden Tornadoes. We never got it quite right, though every Friday Mr. Chervenick tried to inspire us, scampering across the frost-slicked grass in his chocolate leather coat and kid gloves and cordovans to herd us into formation until—in utter disgust —instead of steering a wayward oboe back on course he would simply arrest him or her by the shoulders so the entire block of winds had to stop, and then the brass and the drums, and we would have to start all over again.

Late one Friday in mid-December we were working on the tornado. Dusk had begun to fill the air and it was snowing, but Saturday was our last home game and Mr. Chervenick persuaded the janitor to turn on the lights. An inch or so had fallen during the day and it was impossible to see the lines. "Wrong, wrong, wrong!" Mr. Chervenick shouted. When the girl pulling the xylophone slipped and twisted her ankle, he blew his whistle three times, which meant we were to line up for a final chastising pep talk before we could leave. He climbed the three steps of his little wheeled podium and let us stand in silence for a minute so we would realize how disappointed he was. Snow piled up in our hair. Beyond the sea of flakes drifting through the high lights came the ringing drone of a tractor-trailer's chains on the interstate. In the valley, muffled by a ceiling of clouds, lay the burning grid of Butler, the black river, the busy mills.

"We have all worked very hard this year," he said, and paused, breathing steam, as if speaking to a stadium, waiting for his words to circle. Beside me Warren Hardesty muttered something—a joke, a rejoinder —and then we heard what I immediately identified (from my own .22, my father's Mossberg, the nightly news from Vietnam) as gunshots. A clump of them. They crackled like fireworks, echoed over the bare trees on the other side of the highway. They were close. The band turned to them in unison, something Mr. Chervenick could never get us to do.

It had just turned deer season, and we all knew the power company had a clearcut through there behind the water tower, as well as the rights to the few over-grown fields carved out of the woods, but all of us with guns knew the land was posted, too close to the road and the school. And the time wasn't right for hunting, the light was gone. We looked to each other as if to confirm our surprise.

Mr. Chervenick seemed to understand too, though he was not the hunting type. He praised our dedication, excused us and, instead of leading us back over the footbridge, headed across the empty parking lot for the lit doors of the middle school and stood there rapping on the glass until the janitor let him in.

What we had heard was someone being murdered, someone most of us knew, if dimly. Her name was Annie Marchand, and I knew her first—years before this—merely as Annie the babysitter. Her name at that time was Annie Van Dorn. She lived, then, with her parents, the next house down the road from us. We were not strictly neighbors; between our new hi-ranch and their boxy Greek Revival stretched a mile-wide field Mr. Van Dorn leased to an old farmer named Carlsen. Yet whenever my mother and father decided to escape for dinner out or to a movie, Mr. Van Dorn's truck would pull up at the bottom of our drive and out would pop Annie with her purse and her schoolbooks, ready to whip me at Candyland and train my sister Astrid to draw on eyeliner.

I suspect that at first Astrid was more in love with her than I was. At thirteen Annie was taller than our mother, and strikingly thin. Her red hair came to her waist; her fingers were covered with rings from admirers. She smelled of the Van Dorns' oil furnace and Secret deodorant and Juicy Fruit gum, and she made pizza and sang "Ruby Tuesday" and, for me, "Mr. Big Stuff." Our daydreams, I admit, included her becoming our mother. Once we had an evening-long argument with her over the word "milk," which we—like most Western Pennsylvanians—pronounced "melk," but it did nothing to mediate our crush on her. This went on for years, like a grand affair. She left us only when my sister was old enough to watch me, and by then Annie was out of school and working, and sometimes my mother could not get her for Fridays anyway. We'd see her driving by in her brother Raymond's Maverick or riding behind her boyfriend on his Honda, but rarely. For a few years she became—by her proximity and absence—distant and mysterious. My bedroom faced the field, and at night I studied the yellow eyes of her house and pictured her in her darkened room looking back at me.

Since then she had moved out like her brothers and married and had a girl of her own, but things had not gone well for her. That spring, she and her husband had separated. Mrs. Van Dorn, now widowed, lived alone in the family house. My mother looked in on her every day after work, and often that fall Annie was there, in the kitchen, the two of them commiserating bitterly over coffee. The worst, they must have figured, had already happened.

According to my mother, Mrs. Van Dorn wanted

Annie to move back in with her. Annie and her daughter were living alone above town by the high school. Her house was the only one on Turkey Hill Road, a wooded cul-de-sac that ended at the base of the county water tower. The road had once crossed Old Route 2 but when they laid the interstate the government bought up all the houses and blocked it off on both sides. Beyond a caution-striped guardrail the cracked blacktop wandered off into scrub. The other, unluckier houses were still back there, overgrown, shingles mossy; we used to party in them. Mrs. Van Dorn was worried about Annie's safety, but she and Annie—again, according to my mother—didn't get along well enough to live together, and Annie stayed where she was.

At the hearing her nearest neighbor, Clare Hardesty, said she'd heard the shots and gone to her window. The road was empty, the spotlit water tower half lost in the snow. Annie's lights were on; a colored string blinked around a tree. Clare didn't see any cars that didn't belong, meaning, she explained, the boyfriend's. The two had recently broken up; she would have noticed. When she called, no one answered, so she put on her boots and a wrap and walked down the road. The front door was open, the light spilling out onto the snow. (Here she was asked about footprints, a single broken pane, glass on the bathroom carpet;

she didn't know, she didn't know.) Though the house was empty, something had happened inside. She tried the phone, then ran back to her place to call the state police.

And do you remember noticing, the transcript reads, if the back door was open at this time?

I don't remember, Clare Hardesty answers.

I know—and everyone I grew up with knows—that the back door *was* open and that a pair of tracks led across the backyard and into the woods. We followed them at first in our imaginations, those snowy nights alone in bed (their breath, her bare feet sinking in), and then when the brave had made their pilgrimage, at lunch we hauled on our boots and crossed the interstate and slid down the hill to the spot we as a whole had chosen, just to one side of the board bridge over the spillway of Marsden's Pond. Both the pond and the brook were iced over; only the spillway made noise. The more romantic of the tough girls had placed roses in a vase made of snow, every day a fresh one among the dead. Someone had tramped out a cross, which by January was neatly lined with beer cans. To one side sat a pile of lipsticked cigarette butts and burnt matches like an offering. We stood there, alone or in groups, looking back over the tangle of bare trees beyond which rose the water tower, and below it, invisible, her house. We passed a joint or bowl around

7

and talked about how she was still there in the trees and the creek because the soul never dies. Someone always had gum, and I remember chewing and feeling my jaw harden and thinking that it was true, that I could feel Annie there. But at other times there was nothing, just munchies and a giddiness I would later be ashamed of.

March, cutting class, Warren Hardesty and I walked from the spot all the way to the edge of her backyard, retracing her last steps. It was farther than we thought, and we had to stop to stoke up a roach I'd saved. Warren had some blackberry brandy in a plastic Girl Scout canteen. It was Monday, around third period. The house was for sale but no one was going to buy it. The paint was peeling, the screenporch still full of her junk—lawnchairs, rabbit cages, deflated balls. Warren dared me to cross the lawn and just touch the house.

"You," I said.

"Shit, I live right up the road."

"So?" I said.

We did it together, leaving two sets of bootprints in the perfect snow. We each placed a gloved hand on the porch door. Through a casement window I could see a corner of a rug, and a chair, and light coming through the blue curtains of the front.

"Let's go inside," Warren said.

"Fuck you," I said.

"Pussy," he said, as if there were someone else there judging us.

I dropped my glove to the door handle.

"I'll be right behind you," Warren promised.

The spring protested, rang as if strummed. I stuck my head in. A hose lay coiled beneath a fraying chaise like a snake; above hung a pair of clotheslines, a few grayed pins still clinging. I thought of Annie with a basket of clothes and wondered if she had a dryer or even a washer, because at our old house we—my mother, that is—had always had both, and now we had neither.

Warren pushed me from behind and I fell across a picnic-table bench, knocking over a stack of boxes. One came open and out rolled a yellow mailbox for the *Butler Eagle*. I screamed as if it were a head. Warren was running for the woods, laughing his ass off. I scrambled up and went after him, shouting, "Fucker!"

Later we went back, at first partying at the picnic table and then, when we were more comfortable, in the house itself. We sat on the couch in the chilly living room, passing the canteen, toasting Annie. We never took anyone else and we were careful to clean up after ourselves. We pledged never to take or even move anything. The Prime Directive, Warren called it.

That was me when I was fourteen and I'm not proud of how we treated her place, but now I think I went there because even then I knew I was closer to Annie than all those girls with their roses and the people who went to her funeral. We had history. Stoned, I tried to picture her life there, and her death, though back then that was impossible for me to see clearly. I tried, I suppose, to say goodbye. The house hasn't changed much since then. Eventually someone less reverent broke in and set a fire, and the police boarded it up. It's still there, burnt furniture and all. I've been by.

My mother and I never really talked about what happened. We shared a few words of shocked consolation, and there was an air of mourning about the house, but while the papers were full of accounts, we did not discuss the killing itself, how and why it came about. I now see that she (and myself, though I did not acknowledge it at the time) was going through her own slow tragedy and needed her grief for both herself and me. She still called my father to make sure he would pick me up every other Saturday, but they did not talk beyond money and the logistics of visitation.

We were all seeing a psychiatrist associated with our church, separately, on different days of the week. I remember that Dr. Brady and I mostly discussed hockey, though every session he would ask bluntly how I was doing at home, in school, with the band, with my mother, my father.

"Okay," I told him.

When my mother picked me up, invariably she asked, "Do you think it's helping?"

"I guess," I said.

Astrid, in Tennstaedt, West Germany, with the Air Force, called once a month to see how we were doing and to check up on her bank statement. Her squadron was involved in reconnaissance; "black work," she called it, though we all knew it was just high-altitude photography of Russia. She was putting aside half her pay, wiring it to the Mellon Bank in Butler, and every time my mother drove me in to see Dr. Brady and we passed the branch, I thought of Astrid's money inside, warm as a nest and growing. I thought, desperately, that when her tour was up we could live together in town above the Woolworth's and I could work in the record department. On the phone we talked like hostages. She asked long, impossible questions ("Why do you think they're not talking if they're going to the same guy, and why do you go by yourself?") that under my mother's watchful smile I could only answer with "I don't know." My mother waited until after Christmas to tell her about Annie, and when I got on the phone, Astrid was crying and angry, as if I should have prevented it.

"It's just all going to shit back there, isn't it?"

"I don't know," I said. "I guess."

All my father would say about the killing was that it was a bad business all the way around. He had worked —if briefly—alongside Annie's estranged husband, Glenn. I did not see my father much that winter, and when I did we spoke carefully, like survivors. He would not say a word against or for Glenn Marchand. There was more to it than we had a right to know was my father's position. It was not our affair. To me this was as good as him admitting that he knew the whole story. I wanted him to tell me everything because my mother hadn't and I needed to know. I knew only the rumors and what I could infer from the newspaper, while he had known both parties involved. He did not want to talk about it and I am glad he didn't, for if he had let me know then how he saw the whole thing I probably would not have understood it any more than I understood why he had left my mother.

Once a year I go back to Western Pennsylvania, for Christmas. This year Astrid and I have booked our

flights into Pittsburgh so we can rent a car and drive up
to Butler together, and here we are, cruising through
the snowy country in our big Century. I am comfort-
ably divorced; she is still single. Neither of us mentions these facts. We'll hear them enough when we get
home. Over the years it has become a bit of a ritual for
me to drive by our old house and stop to contemplate
it. It's a form of stalling, of warming up for the hard
part.

"Can we?" I say.

Astrid says nothing, but reluctantly slows and pulls
onto the cinder berm. All fall we've talked on the
phone, and she knows I need a little indulgence.

We sit in the warmth of the car with the radio off.
The shrubs have grown up and filled out around the
foundation, but the house itself hasn't changed much.
Astrid thinks it's the siding. On the roof stands a faded
Santa, waving. The new people are doing all right. In
the last year they've added an aboveground pool; it
sleeps under a blue tarpaulin. I've seen their boy
shooting hoops on the drive, and once a daughter
shoveling. But what about the inside, is it any different
—the tree, the smell of turkey all afternoon while on
TV the football games change? We sit in the car and I
imagine our father in the basement rec room, lying on
the couch under an afghan, his ashtray on the shag rug.

A razor commercial jangles, the baseboard heaters clink. The Steelers are beating someone but he is asleep, and our mother shoos us upstairs.

"Seen enough?" Astrid asks, and when I don't answer shifts into drive. I will never stop being the baby; all the decisions are hers.

Carlsen's field is mud and stubble. Every Christmas our mother marvels that he is still alive, guiding his glass-cabbed Deere over the furrows. A mile off, the Van Dorns' rises.

It is here, between, as we approach their house, that the past reaches me. On both sides lie nothing but fields, snow in the ditches, telephone poles. A windbreak of old oaks waves around the house. Astrid doesn't slow, though I turn from her. The second son, Dennis, is in it now; the side yard is clogged with his projects. Beside a pair of school district vans a camper sits on cinder blocks, beside it a snowmobile, a fat stack of tractor tires. In back leans a small barn, doorless, a car peeking its nose out like a mouse—Raymond's old Maverick. The house, like ours, betrays little, but the paint is new, and the tin roof and quaint lace curtains. From the porch flies a rainbowed fish windsock, defying the season. I will have to remember that. And then we are past, shooting between the drifted fields. I turn in my harness to watch the house diminish, and Astrid sighs.

"Are we going to go through this again?" she says.

"No," I say, "I'm all done with that."

She looks at me as if to say I'm not fooling anyone, then turns back to the road.

"I guess I should just forget it, right?" We've had this argument forever.

"I'm not saying you should forget it," Astrid says. "Just stop going over it. Let it rest for once. One year."

"Right," I say. "This'll be the last year. Promise."

She snorts and shakes her head, gives up on me. I say this every year, but what if this year it's true?

Behind us the two houses are blips in the mirror, dots on the horizon, and as we speed along the empty fields they drift with the dwindling perspective and line up like the sights on a rifle, become one.

Today, after we say hello and get settled, our mother will ask one of us to run out to the store, and before giving me the keys, Astrid will look at me as if to say, I know where you're going. I will sit a few minutes under the water tower while the snow falls and later tell my mother I had to go all the way into town.

I don't like coming home. It keeps me from being nostalgic, which by nature I am. Even before the plane begins its descent, I find myself dreading the questions left unanswered by my childhood. Annie. My parents. My own lost years. I know that once we touch down I will not be able to think clearly, that every remembered Pizza Hut and body shop, every stretch of road I know intimately, will stun me like love.

The plane I take goes right over Butler. Fifty miles out of Pittsburgh, the pilot drops down under the clouds and I can find the city. It is not much, the downtown clumped around the Main Street section of Route 8, then the bridge, the train tracks snaking with the Connoquenessing, the blue blocks of the Armco mill. Cars crawl up the long hill. I am looking for the aqua dot of the water tower, though it is always some other landmark that jumps out. The mall that used to be new. The post office depot with its rows of Jeeps. The Home for Crippled Children—now the Rehabilitation Center—where my mother still works. Roads crisscross and connect; woods neatly part to let the power lines through. This high up, I feel as if the place I was raised is not such a mystery. Looking down at the farms and fields, the two schools separated by the interstate, the black bean of Marsden's Pond, I think that, like my sister putting Russia together piece by piece, if I concentrate on the details I will be able to make sense of the whole, that I will finally understand everything that happened back then, when I know that I can't.

T W O

GLENN MARCHAND SLAPS HIMSELF in the mirror, watches the nick fill with blood. He's already shaved once today, for church, and still has on his good shoes and best dark slacks. His good white shirt and the maroon paisley tie Annie gave him for Christmas last year hang from the bathroom doorknob, safe from the Barbasol and splashing hot water. The Hai Karate was a gift from her too, a birthday, he can't remember when, but it's safe, she likes it. It stings like a bugger in the cut. Trying to be too fine, Glenn thinks. He tears off a corner of toilet paper to stanch the bleeding.

"Don't want to be late," his father calls from the bedroom doorway. Glenn finds him in the mirror and waves over his shoulder.

Frank Marchand rests against the jamb and watches his son leaning over the sink, mouth open, trying to position the tiny triangle with his fingers. Glenn has been home for three months now, and isn't working. He goes to the fires but otherwise Frank has no idea what he does with his time. Drives around the county. Drinks with his buddy Rafe. Sleeps. The bedroom is a mess, like a child's; shirts and shoes and 8-track tapes cover the hardwood floor along with bits of Bomber's chew toys and rawhide bones, all drifted with clumps of dog hair. The room smells of Bomber, who right now is outside in his new house, banished since this morning, when in a frenzy of gratitude he knocked Olive against the kitchen table and spilled everyone's juice. Frank goes to the window. Bomber seems comfortable enough, paws crossed, his husky's face split with a perpetual grin. A cold October rain drips from the trees, the light painting the sheets of the unmade bed gray. A Bible lies open on the night table, passages underlined in red pen. On a chair in a dark corner sits a plush bunny Glenn has bought for Tara, a red ribbon around its neck, its arms open as if ready to hug someone. It is nearly the size of Tara, and Frank does not want to think what it cost.

Every other Sunday it's the same thing. Frank is not Glenn's natural father, but that does not stop this from hurting him. Tara is their only grandchild who lives in the state, and Glenn is their youngest. Our baby, Olive still calls him, and it's true, Glenn has never taken to the world like Richard and Patty. He has a talent for both finding and, lately, losing jobs. Part of it is his charm, the utter optimism he projects. He has a gift for ingratiating himself—like his natural father, Frank thinks, a pleasant, truly harmless man who the last they knew was doing five-to-fifteen in Minnesota for bilking retired couples out of their pension money. Frank has tried to help, lining Glenn up with people he knows. They all like Glenn at first, and then he starts coming in late and calling in sick and doing a half-assed job when he does come in—Frank's heard it all. It's baffling; Frank knows he's a good worker. The kid's heartsick, his friends down at the Elks tell him, give him time. Olive thinks Glenn would be a natural for sales; he looks good in clothes, he's smart and he likes people. He does like people, Frank agrees, but Glenn has always seemed more clever than smart to him, and as for his looks, Frank's no judge when it comes to men. What he loved about Glenn as a boy he now finds tiresome—his even temper, his unshakable faith that things will turn out fine in the end. It's all false now, gone sour. It's not just the separation, but recently Frank has had him anchoring hose instead of on rescue like usual. In the clinch Glenn is tentative, and that can get people killed. Frank doesn't understand what is happening, why this son of his is falling apart at the first run of bad luck. He is willing to take some of the blame but not all; part of it is the new church Glenn's been going to since he tried to kill himself—the Lakeview New Life Assembly. It's in a prefab with a ten-foot wood steeple wired on top, and just a step above snakehandling. Frank doesn't understand—he and Olive raised them all solid Presbyterian. Olive says it's all right, it's the only good thing in his life anymore, the only thing that keeps him going. She blames it all on Annie. Frank is tempted but resists; he's always liked her. *She* was the one thing Glenn had going for him.

Glenn has the blowdryer on high. From downstairs Olive calls up, "One-fifteen!"

"It's one-fifteen," Frank hollers.

Glenn dries his hair another minute as if he hasn't heard, then stops and starts working on his shirt.

Frank picks his way through the mess and leans in the bathroom door. "How are you doing for cash?"

"I'm all right," Glenn says, but stops buttoning.

Frank pulls out his wallet, licks a finger and leafs through his bills. "Why don't you take her out for a treat on her grandad." He gives Glenn a twenty, knowing he'll pocket the change.

"Thanks," Glenn says. He checks his watch and turns to the mirror to do his tie. Frank points out a dab of shaving cream in his sideburn and Glenn wipes it away.

"Where are you taking her today?"

"The lake. Maybe out to the mall. The picture people are there this weekend."

"Well, you have a good time."

"We always do," Glenn says with such spirit that Frank wants to sit him down and tell him it's all right, nobody blames him for what has happened.

Glenn can't get the tie the right length and wishes his father would stop lurking. He understands he's worried; yesterday Glenn talked with Gary Sullivan over at the salvage yard, and he all but promised him a job. When Glenn first came home his mother and father were on him about not working; now they've stopped asking. During the week they hardly pay attention to him, then Sundays treat him like he's up for some award. At dinner they quiz him, then, disappointed, watch "Columbo" in silence the rest of the night. He's going to get this job and keep it, he can feel it. He's better now. He's ready.

Finally he gets the knot right and buttons the wings of his collar. He peels the piece of paper off his chin. It's not good but good enough; he's already late. His father trails him downstairs like a bodyguard.

His jacket's on the back of the kitchen door. Nearly one-thirty. Annie will be pissed; her mother wanted her to do some shopping.

Glenn's mother comes in from the football game to see him off. She smooths the arms of his jacket, picks at lint. "Say hello for us."

"I will," Glenn says, jingling his keys.

"Now you remind Tara that next time she's seeing her grandma and grandad."

"I will," he says, too hard, and he's sorry. His father offers him an umbrella, an old Totes Glenn gave them years ago, and Glenn guiltily accepts it. His mother wants a kiss, so he bends down and turns his cheek to her powdery mouth. "I've got to go," he says.

"Then go," his father says, opening the back door to a humid gust. "Don't let us old folks slow you down."

They stand in the screenporch, watching him cross the yard to Bomber's house. Glenn has a new blue bandana for him, and Bomber rattles the chain. The rain has let up some. The yard is heaped with wet leaves. Olive knows Glenn will come home heart-broken, and while it is his own fault for not seeing what his wife is, she can't help but wish things were different. She thinks of the picture Richard sent of his new house in Tucson, Debbie and Becky beside him in the driveway, smiling and tanned. In back they have a pool. Richard has sent them a pair of tickets to visit at Christmas, and though they'll go, Olive doesn't feel right about leaving Glenn home alone.

"I don't know what to do for him," she says, arms crossed to stay warm.

"Nothing," Frank says. "He's not a child."

"I know," she says.

He puts an arm around her as Bomber, set free, leaps onto the tailgate of Glenn's truck. The bed is littered with cans, and Bomber kicks them around. Glenn waves as he gets in the cab. They wave back as if he's leaving for good.

He revs the engine, and Olive sloughs off Frank's arm.

"I'm cold," she says, and goes inside, leaving Frank to watch him off alone. The exhaust comes out in white clouds. The trees drip, Bomber prances. Just as Glenn slips it in gear, Frank remembers the gift in his room.

"The rabbit," Frank calls, trying to flag him, "you forgot the rabbit," but his son is late and thinks he is waving, wishing him luck.

Glenn realizes on the interstate, approaching the exit for the high school. He whacks the dashboard and shakes his head. "You idiot."

The day is ruined for him. He doesn't see the point of going through with it. He needs everything to be perfect and he can't even get the easy things right. Just once, he thinks, please. He dreams—though no longer believes—that at the end of one of these Sunday visits Annie will ask him to stay for dinner and maybe some TV, a few drinks. Things will lead to things and who knows, maybe he'll stay the night, and the next, and the next, and things will be back to the way they were. They have been separated almost eight months now, and not once has this happened. They have taken Tara on picnics together, and to her swimming clinic at the lake this summer, and Annie in the past few weeks has been relatively pleasant toward him, but Sundays he has become accustomed to driving home alone, angry he could even consider a reconciliation. All week he has been priming himself to accept defeat, but to fail before he has even set foot in her door is crushing.

He slows coming up the ramp and turns onto Burdon Hollow Road. Bomber smiles in the rearview mirror, his fur blowing. Any other day Glenn would have him in the cab, but he'd ruin his suit. It's not so cold, just wet underfoot. From the bridge he can see clouds filling the valley, half masking the sprawl of town. When they were going out, he and Annie used to park behind the high school and look down at the lights. Now the cops cruise through there and the kids use the lake.

"Prettier there anyway," he admits.

He makes the turn onto Far Line, automatically checking to see if anyone's nose is poking out of the middle school drive. It's strange now how well he knows the roads yet is mystified by his old home, his wife, his child. The trees are black with rain. He checks his chin in the mirror—acceptable. Annie didn't even come see him in the hospital. The only person he's really talked with about the attempt is Elder Francis, who says surrendering to a greater mercy was necessary for Glenn to be truly saved. Eventually he was, but first by the county paramedics. His friends from Engine 3 had to chop down the door to the apartment. His father was there watching them work on him. Glenn could see him above the dipping heads, wanted to talk to him, apologize, but the Seconal had already started to work, and the distance between them ran liquid and oppressively heavy, as if he were looking up from the bottom of a creek. When he opened his mouth fingers gripped his tongue. He doesn't like to think about it, it was a long time ago, it was stupid.

As he brakes for Turkey Hill he glances over at Clare Hardesty's, expecting her at the window, noting his arrival. The curtains are drawn but that's no guarantee she isn't peeking out at him. He waves, just to make sure.

And then he is faced with his old home, the white Cape sitting lonely at the end of the road. The woods are so dark that the single streetlight is on. The water tower looms blue and giant. He pulls into the drive behind Annie's Maverick and hops out, careful of the puddles. The rain's barely coming down here. She's already put up Halloween decorations—cardboard cats and jack-o'-lanterns taped to the windows, a wide-eyed scarecrow for the door. Her family was big on holidays. Again, he thinks of the bunny and shakes his head. In back, Bomber is getting frantic, knocking the cans around.

"You don't jump," Glenn warns, then says, "out," and Bomber goes over the side and bolts past him for the door, spattering his pants with mud. Glenn wipes at it with a hand, then gives up. Before knocking, he thinks next time he ought to bring flowers. He'll tell her about the job.

He has had all week, but as she opens the door to him, Glenn finds he is not prepared to see Annie. Her height is surprising, the color of her hair, as if he has remembered her dimly, like an old photo that doesn't do its subject justice. She has a faded pair of Levi's on, and a thermal undershirt, and her new glasses. Her face is a mess of red lines—sleeping on the couch, she confesses; they've both been sick—but when she smiles at Bomber, Glenn is defenseless and so touched that he is angry with himself and, for different reasons, her.

"You're late," she says, kidding, but waits for him to explain.

"Church."

"Tara," she calls, "your father's here," and in the minute it takes her to wander in from the bedroom, they stand there. Glenn regroups. He interrogates the furniture, picks up signals from the half-read *Mademoiselle* lying on the couch, the crayons piled like deadfall. The TV plays a bad movie, people being stalked down dark hospital corridors.

"How are your folks?" Annie asks.

"Sick of me. Your mom?"

"Good."

"Good."

Tara appears and gives them an excuse not to talk. She hugs a stuffed Winnie-the-Pooh to her chest. Bomber almost knocks her down; Glenn claps once and he sits, twice and he lies down. Glenn has never seen the overalls Tara has on, red corduroy with a kangaroo on the pocket. He kneels down to admire them and receive a hug. She smells like grape cough syrup.

"Mommy made it," she says.

"They're very pretty," Glenn says. "Where would you like to go with your old dad today? Would you like to go to the mall and have your picture taken?"

"No."

"Okay, where *would* you like to go—the lake?"

"Don't ask her," Annie says, "just tell her. And take boots if you're going to be outside."

"I want to go Grammy's," Tara says.

"No, honey," Annie says, "you and Daddy are going to the mall. Mommy has to go to the store for Grammy."

"I want to go to the store," Tara says, glowering.

"We get to go to the mall," Glenn says, trying to be cheery, "with the horse and the rocket ship." He takes her hand but she snatches it back.

"I don't want Daddy. I want Mommy."

"Just grab her," Annie says, putting her own shoes on. "She'll scream and cry for five minutes, then she'll be fine. She loves having her picture taken —don't you, babe? Sure. She's just cranky because of the ear infection." She hauls her coat on. "Is Winnie-the-Pooh going with you?"

Glenn holds his hand out.

"Come on, pumpkin," Annie coaxes, and still frowning, Tara takes it.

"Four-thirty," Glenn says outside, over the hood.

"Make it five if you want," Annie says. "I've got errands to run." She folds herself into the Maverick and pulls out while he is trying to buckle Winnie-the-Pooh in with Tara. The rain has inexplicably stopped. They'll go to the mall and then the lake if it's cleared off. In back, Bomber is pouncing on a can like a wolf toying with a mouse.

Glenn starts the engine and backs out onto the road and thinks of Annie opening the door to him. That first instant, did she actually smile because of him? He sees her kneeling to pet Bomber, strands of her hair catching in his coat. For a moment his head goes completely empty, trying to make space for the memory, unsure if he wants to or not. The water tower grows in the rearview mirror. Beside him Tara is playing with the buckle of the other seat belt, clicking the button as if it's a phaser and making shooting noises. She looks up at him and fires.

"Are you having fun with your big dad," Glenn says, "or what?"

Annie's mother, May, is waiting for her with a list of groceries and what she says is enough money to cover everything.

"If it isn't," May says at the door, "you can get rid of the Lorna Doones. I like them with my coffee in the middle of the afternoon, especially this time of year, but I don't absolutely have to have them."

"Ditch the Lorna Doones," Annie says, and makes a mark beside it. It's a game they play; she'll buy them with her own money if she has to. She worries about her mother staying here alone, especially lately. She seems thinner, and after heating water for their coffee sometimes leaves the burner on.

"When will you be back?"

"Whenever I get back," Annie says. "Around dinner. I've got to stop by the mall and run a bunch of errands."

"How is Glenn?"

"Fine."

"Say hello to him for me if you would."

"I do," Annie says, "all the time."

"I just wish," May starts, and then sighs.

"Ma," Annie says, "forget it."

"I just wish the two of you were happy."

"I'm going. I'll be back when I get back." She crosses the porch and takes the three stairs down to the walk with a skip that makes May remember her as a child. Even then no one could talk to her. She was famous for quitting games and playing by herself. Charles worried that she wouldn't have any friends, that with her pride and temper she would end up alone. May's glad he's not around to see his prediction come true.

"Lorna Doones," May calls after her.

"Lorna Doones," Annie says, waving the list over her shoulder, but she doesn't look back.

The only thing perishable is the milk, and the weather's cold enough, Annie hopes, that she can leave it in the trunk. The fields roll, dead wind-combed corn, white as bone. She is driving the back way through Renfrew so she doesn't have to go past the country club. It's not like Barb might figure out what's going on between her and Brock just from seeing the

Maverick, but they have to be careful. It's hard enough as it is. Annie will see her tonight as the shifts change. For ten or fifteen minutes they'll be at the same table in the break room, sharing cigarettes and laughing, glad that at least one of them is done for the day. Barb wants her to come over; they haven't seen each other much since Barb started working lunch at the Rusty Nail. Annie keeps putting her off, saying she's busy with Tara. "Bring her," Barb says. "I really need to talk to someone. Really."

Annie keeps looking for Barb's yellow Bug, expects it at every crossroads. She's not good at this. Brock is only her second since Glenn left. The first was someone from work, one of the summer help, a kid. It was one night, and worth it. She was just testing herself. This is different, weird, unreal. Barb was her maid of honor. Barb helped her get the job at the club. She and Brock have only been seeing each other for three weeks now but their affair has erased chunks of Annie's past. It seems to her that she has always been a false friend, a slut; whatever punishment Barb chooses for her will be too lenient.

Yet at the same time, shooting along the empty blacktop with the Allmans whooping it up at the end of "Ramblin' Man" and the sun beginning to peek out of the clouds, this is the happiest she's been in years.

The last time they made love was in Barb's apartment, last Sunday while she was working brunch at the club. Brock wanted to use the bed, but Annie convinced him it would be more fun in the bathroom. It was a joke between them; the first time they did it was against the sink, at a party he and Barb threw. The keg was in the tub and Annie was wearing navy. She and Brock were talking as they refilled their cups, and then they were kissing—she could see herself in his arms in the mirror—and Brock locked the door and lifted her up onto the wet edge of the Formica. It was funny how it hadn't frightened her when people knocked; last week every little sound from the hall had her grabbing for her clothes. When Brock suggested a motel she didn't think he was serious. It's still a joke to her, something out of an old movie, but she appreciates it. They don't want to hurt Barb.

The place is at the south end of the county, off Route 8—Susan's Motel. Waterbeds, color. It's in back of a house crowned with TV antennae, half hidden from the road. Annie has passed it millions of times, has heard her mother remark upon it. She has to get in the middle lane to take the left and feels the eyes of the other drivers on her. The No-tell Motel. She beats a tractor-trailer across and zips up the drive and into the back, invisible again.

The parking lot is nearly full—and on a Sunday, she thinks. Football widows. Around the side are spaces for big rigs. All the cars are backed in so you can't read their license plates; Annie finds herself memorizing the cars themselves. The number's almost comforting. Brock's Charger is parked in front of Room 9. She backs in beside it, locks up and puts her keys in her purse.

The first thing that hits her is how empty it looks, how dead. There are no lawn chairs, no Pepsi machines, just glass on the walk, weeds in the cracks. The gutters are rusting. The curtains are drawn across every window but the office. Behind her, over the house, comes the whine of the highway. The door to 9 has a peephole and a steel plate riveted around the knob. Annie knocks. A car turns into the drive and suddenly she wishes she had tucked her hair up under a hat or worn a scarf. She wants to turn just to prove to herself that it's not Barb, that she's being foolish, but can't. The door is dented, as if someone tried to kick it down. What kind of a person is she becoming? The car idles behind her, looking for a spot. She knocks again, harder, but the door is opening, it's Brock, everything's all right.

————

They're into the second bottle of wine and Brock can't believe how good the TV reception is. It's snowing in Bloomington, Minnesota, and Fran Tarkenton is scrambling. The heater stirs the curtains, a crack of light sifting into the black room. They lie naked on top of the covers, sated, resting the bathroom glasses on their chests. Her long body, the smell of her shampoo. At times like these he thinks he can leave Barb—that he will—when he knows it's not true. He's been trying to come up with a way to tell Annie it's not going to work. They both know they're only postponing it.

He doesn't think he's in love with her, but how can he be sure? He and Barb hardly talk anymore. At night he tries but she's tired, can't he wait till morning? He lies there listening to her snore—and yet in everyone's eyes she'd be the wronged one. Annie listens to him, gives him the attention he needs. All Barb seems interested in is when he gets paid next. It would be easier if he didn't know how close Annie and Barb are. Even now Brock knows Annie is thinking about her, that after the flush of love cools she will ask how they are getting along, as if her first responsibility is keeping them together.

"All right," he says when she finally does, but he can't hide his annoyance. This is supposed to be their time alone. He's been dreaming of it all week; his patients at the Overlook Home know something's up, tease him for being happy. He listens to their stories of long-ago loves, Paris in the twenties, the war in Spain. Will his life ever be that exciting?

"I worry about her," Annie says.

"She's not going to know," he says, impatient, then regrets it.

"I don't know why I'm here."

"Are we going to go through this again?"

"I'm sorry. Everything's been so nice. I don't know why I always have to ruin things."

"Don't apologize," Brock says. The Steelers intercept and while he's watching the runback he misses what Annie is saying.

"What?" he says.

"Forget it."

"Tell me."

She gets up and goes to the bathroom, closes the door and turns on the shower. Brock looks at the door, looks back at the game and sighs. He finishes his wine and gets up to kill the TV and for an instant sees himself in the mirror, the colored rush of the play painting his body, and wonders how he got himself into this. He thinks of Glenn Marchand—how only a fool would let her go—and takes the bottle from the ice bucket and follows her into the steaming bathroom.

The photographer says they make a lovely couple. For thirty-five dollars, Glenn says, he hopes so. Tara rides the motorcycle twice; he's not going to fight her. When they get outside the sky is clear and they agree on the playground. Bomber's been waiting patiently.

"Fifteen minutes," Glenn promises him.

Glenn's father and Glenn's real father were born under the lake, and every time he drives alongside it (or at church, gazing out the big picture window behind the altar), Glenn thinks of the town down there, the streets and houses and farms the park service bought up. It's still on some maps—Gibbsville. His father has a fat album of pictures. Glenn remembers him taking the whole family out to where the old road disappeared under softly lapping water, the double yellow lines wavy. He remembers seeing a steeple in the distance, only the tip visible, but in the pictures it's too far away. Sometimes Glenn takes the album up to his room and walks through the town, past the house his parents lived in, the store they say his real father robbed. His walk always ends with his new family standing in the middle of the road, the water rising behind them. Why, Glenn thinks, are these people smiling?

The woman and the little boy they usually see at
the playground are there, and Glenn makes Bomber
stay in the truck. The sun's out, blazing off the lake,
but there are puddles beneath the swings and at the
bottom of the slide. Tara sits while Glenn struggles
with her boots.

"Do you remember the lady's name?" he asks her
on a long shot. Every time he has to remind her. "Do
you remember the little boy's name?"

"I think his name is Eric." She has trouble with
her r's. It's common but everything worries Glenn.
When he was a boy friends teased him about his ears,
and now he wears his hair over them.

"His name is Steven," Glenn corrects.

The woman's is Nan. She's older, divorced, from
town. Her husband got custody because she was an
alcoholic, like Glenn's birth mother. In spring when
he first came here with Tara they traded histories, as if
they were dating. When he was in the hospital she sent
him a card that said, "I didn't think you were a quitter." Now they speak easily, pacing the grass or sitting
at a picnic table while their children race from the
jungle gym to the balance beam.

"Bomber's okay," Nan offers, but Glenn says he
can wait.

"Look at him, he's sad."

"He's fine."

"You look nice," Nan notes. "As usual. How's Annie?"

"Better," Glenn says, glad to share the news with her.

Nan wants details.

"I don't know. The last few weeks she's been a lot nicer. I don't know why." He shrugs and she looks at him and he can feel himself blushing. "I might have a job."

"Hey," Nan says, giving his wrist a squeeze, "that's really good."

Annie goes home the back way, the drawn orange light of the dying afternoon shooting through the windows. She's sore and her head beats with the wine. She keeps the radio off, trying to think. She hates this time of day, when the sky deepens and she knows she has to go to work and leave Tara with Clare or her mother. The thought of the motel disgusts her, the cinder block walls and bright, tiny bathroom. Right now someone is coming in to clean up after them, to strip the beds and spray Lysol on everything. At the club Barb is freshening coffees for the last remaining bridge players. Annie chews a stick of gum and punches the lighter in. There's an old pack of Winstons in the glove compartment, a few doglegged stragglers left. Her mother thinks she's quit completely, so she has to roll down her window to smoke. It's stale but she drags on it hard, lets the first cloud out like a sigh.

She is going to stop seeing Brock—not that they were ever together. She comes to this decision each time she leaves him, but this time she means it. He's not helping her. She still has to face the bills by herself, and take care of Tara and the house. She's tired of coming home to nothing. Maybe her mother is right when she says she needs someone—meaning Glenn. He's changed, her mother says, and while Annie agrees, she isn't sure she likes those changes. She's not sure what becoming a Born Again means, only that he's even nicer, more polite—two things about him she never did appreciate. What are her choices? Brock is not permanent, Annie doesn't expect him to be. Barb ought to at least know that about him by now.

It's easy to think like this by herself in the car, but when she sees the one-mile marker of the Parkinsons' house, her new resolutions evaporate. She slows and flips the butt out the window and chews another stick of gum. Her mother has the porch light on and, suddenly paranoid, Annie imagines someone has stolen her groceries from the trunk.

They're still there, just spilled, the colonist on the

front of the Quaker Oats box smiling reassuringly. The milk is cool to the touch.

"Steelers won," her mother greets her from the porch. She is wearing slippers, and Annie wonders when she was out of the house last. Her father's old Polara lists in the driveway, one front tire flat.

"You figured they would."

"How was the mall?"

"Crowded."

"It's the rain."

Annie carries the two bags into the kitchen and helps her mother put them away. The fridge is nearly empty. The door is heavy with condiments, but on the top shelf sit only a brick of butter, a tray of eggs and a carton of OJ.

"Ma, do you have bread?"

Her mother doesn't answer.

Annie opens the tin on the counter. Just crusts. "Ma."

"It's all right," May says, trying to play it down. She thought she'd put it on the list. "I'll ask Louise to pick some up for me."

"Mrs. Parkinson is busy. She can't be running around doing errands for you."

"She says she doesn't mind."

"You have to eat," Annie says.

"I eat."

"What are you having for dinner?"

"I really haven't given it a thought," May says. "There's chicken in the freezer."

"Come home with me. You can watch Tara there and I'll drive you home in the morning."

"I'll have to get dressed."

"Please," Annie says. "Ma, c'mon."

In the car her mother says, "You never get rid of the smell, do you?"

The sun is down by the time Glenn turns onto Turkey Hill, and the spotlight throws shadows of catwalks and guywires into the trees behind the water tower. Annie's home. This is the hard part of Sunday, dropping Tara off. He pulls in behind the Maverick and kills the truck, but instead of helping her with her belt, he just sits there. Bomber's excited, thinking he's home.

"Did you have fun today?" Glenn asks her.

"Yes."

"Good." He ruffles her hair, taps the tip of her nose as if his finger is a wand. "Next time we're going to see Grandma and Grandad, all right?"

"Aw wight."

"You know I love you."

"Yes."

He wants more, but it is enough. He doesn't want to drive home crying like last time. It's the antidepressants; they get him going like a yo-yo.

"Okay," he says, and undoes her belt. "Come out my side, and watch the step down."

They walk to the door together. She still won't hold his hand. "You ring it," he says.

For the second time today he is stunned by the person opening his own door—Annie's mother, whom he hasn't seen since helping set up for the Women's Auxiliary dish-to-pass a month ago. May likes him, he's always thought, because Annie's father was a fireman. When Glenn first came to in the hospital, she was there with his parents; she apologized for Annie, which he thought she didn't have to do.

"Come in," May says, "it must be getting chilly out there," and starts to help Tara off with her coat. Tara jerks away, scowling. "Little Miss Independence."

The house is warm with cooking. Annie's on the couch watching TV, ignoring him.

"What's the occasion?" Glenn asks May.

"Your wife thinks I'm starving to death."

"I do not," Annie says without taking her eyes off the TV.

"We're having chicken à la king. There's enough if you'd like to stay."

It seems to Glenn that the room has gone silent. Annie looks at them as if they've said something wrong in front of Tara.

"I don't know if I'm allowed."

"Why not?" May says.

"Sure," Annie says, "why not? All my other wonderful relatives are here."

When Glenn asks her out, Annie can't believe he's serious. It's not like him to put her on the spot. She can't tell if he's desperate or confident. He looks good.

"Neutral territory," he says. "Just for dinner, nothing else. Your choice, any place in town."

"Sounds inviting," her mother says.

"Let me think about it," Annie says, stalling, trying to brush it off.

She's forgotten how well he speaks, how pleasant he can be. She has to remind herself that half of what he's saying isn't true. He says he has a new job over at Sullivan's Salvage, but Mr. Parkinson works there, and surely her mother would have heard from Mrs. Parkinson if it had actually happened. Still, it's fascinating to watch how he gets himself going, how he cheers himself along. Her mother keeps looking at her to make sure she's listening.

She isn't really. She's still trying to absorb the four of them here at her kitchen table. Usually it's just her, rushed for time and pleading with Tara to eat. She's having a hard time admitting that she likes having them —him—here, especially after such a strange day. His suit reminds her of when they were dating and he used to come over to their place for supper. His manners impressed her parents, and his hair. Her mother still hasn't changed her opinion. Annie knows she blames the separation on her; she's never stopped defending Glenn. Once, in the only full-fledged argument they've had about it, her mother asked, ''What did he do?'' and Annie could only say, ''Nothing. He doesn't do anything, that's the problem.'' Her mother doesn't understand. She never says it, but in every conversation they have about her problems with Glenn, her mother implies that Annie is hurting her father, which would be ridiculous except that at heart Annie believes it. She did not want the separation, neither of them did. She wants Tara to have a father, and Glenn can be a good father, but at this time last year he was out of work and resented watching Tara while she pulled the day shift at Friendly's. It was bullshit. She'd come home and he'd be on the couch, well into his third beer, and the house would be a mess and he'd expect her to get dinner and do the dishes and weekends run out to the laundry.

"Everyone else does it," her mother said then. "I did it for your father and all three of you kids for thirty years, and I survived."

"I know," Annie said, trying to show her she saw her side, but knowing now that she would have to do it alone.

Things have changed since then, Annie thinks, looking around the table. I've changed. She watches Glenn trying to smile as he chews his seconds and wonders what she is going to do with him. She has never questioned that he loves her—or not in the way that she wonders about Brock. He's devoted. That's the hardest thing to admit, that if she took him back he would do everything he could for her.

"I ordered four sets of prints," Glenn is telling her mother, "one for everyone."

"Let me pay you. I insist."

"Yes," Annie says.

Glenn holds up his hand to stop them. "You can pay for the next set." He puts his hand on his heart. "These are from me."

"Well, thank you," her mother says, impressed again, and looks to Annie.

"Thank you, Glenn."

"No problem," he says, "now how about that dinner?"

"I've got work every day next week," she says, though her mother knows she has Thursday off.

"Lunch?"

Annie looks around the table; no one is going to save her. She can think of a thousand things she needs to do—work on Tara's Halloween costume, finish the ironing, clean the bathroom—but none sounds like a good enough excuse. Barb wants her to come over. She thinks of the dented door, the first stale hit of the Winston.

"I'll watch Tara," her mother volunteers.

"Okay," Annie says, as if she's convinced her, "I guess lunch couldn't hurt."

Glenn wants to stay and do the dishes, but Annie says it's time for him to leave. She has to get ready for work. Though he's been picturing himself at the sink, washing while she dries, he doesn't argue. He helps clear, then lifts Tara over his head, turns her upside down and runs around the living room holding her by the ankles. Bomber follows.

"Remember she just ate," Annie warns.

He drops Tara onto the couch like a bomb, and she laughs, her face puffed with blood.

"I want to ride again," she demands.

"Next time," he says. "Daddy's got to go."

"I don't want you to."

Glenn looks to the kitchen, hoping Annie's heard, but there's only May, saving the peas for tomorrow. Annie's probably getting dressed. He's seen her in the new uniform once or twice before—a plain gray skirt and white blouse with a maroon apron and plastic nametag. She always looks good to him.

"I don't want to go either," he tells Tara, "but I'll be back. Okay?"

"Okay."

"Give me a kiss. And a hug. Who's a big bug?"

"Daddy."

"Say goodbye to Bomber."

She puts the dog in a headlock and, closing her eyes, buries her face in his fur.

Annie comes in wearing her uniform and black pantyhose, searching for her work shoes—white like a nurse's. Glenn spots one sticking out from beneath the couch, reaches under the ruffle and finds the other. Annie thanks him and sits down on the couch to put them on. He kneels there between her and Tara and Bomber, and thinks that it is too early, that though he

wants to, he's not ready to propose to his whole family
—that they're not ready to say yes.

At the door he reminds Annie not to forget their
lunch.

"How could I," she says, as if it's a chore, but
doesn't try to back out. May gives him a kiss. It's dark
out, and wintry, trees tapping their branches. The
guywires hum. Bomber marks the stem of the
mailbox, then waits for him to lower the tailgate.
Glenn waves before getting in. He flips his lights on
and they have to shade their eyes. Pulling away, he
honks.

He punches in a tape and—what luck he suddenly
has—it's Cat Stevens singing, *Oooh baby baby it's a wild
world. It's hard to get by just upon a smile.* The song seems
wise to Glenn tonight, and he cruises past the middle
school and down Far Line at half his usual speed, savoring the view of town, the valley shimmering in the
cold like embers. His parents will wonder why he's
late.

"The heck with 'Columbo,' " Glenn says, and
when the track ends he clicks the program button
three times so he can hear it again. He turns it up on
the interstate, under the orange mercury-vapor lamps,
and croons along with Cat. It ends and he's about to
cue it up again when in the strobing light of a clover-
leaf he sees Winnie-the-Pooh lying in the muddy foot-

well under the dash. He reaches over, driving blind for an instant, and picks it up. By some miracle it's clean, just a dried patch on one paw that brushes right off. Cat's started his next song, riding the peace train, going home again. Glenn holds the soft bear to his cheek, presses his nose into the fur and, closing his eyes, inhales.

T H R E E

THE NIGHT BEFORE my father left us, he packed the few things he would need at his new place. My mother kept to the rec room, doing laundry and watching TV, something British on the educational station. It was a schoolnight, a Tuesday, because I was in bed, listening to "Radio Mystery Theatre" on my little transistor. My father by then was sleeping in my sister's room, beside mine, though sometimes—I knew—he crossed the hall after they decided I was asleep. Through the wall I could hear hangers pinging, the screek and thump of drawers.

I knew there would not be a fight. That summer we had been through the screaming and the crying and the silence. Driving home from the family Fourth of July picnic at my grandparents' camp, my mother struck my father in the face—just once, openhanded. I had been sneaking Rolling Rock ponies from my uncle John's ice chest all afternoon, and sat in the backseat, woozy, watching the dotted line scroll out of the dark, so that when she smacked him it seemed fuzzy and unreal. I did not suddenly become sober, only more removed, yet now I saw them clearly, turned to each other while the road poured heedlessly under our car. My father grabbed my mother's wrists and pushed her against the opposite door. The Country Squire swerved over the line. He needed both hands to right it.

The violence must have frightened them as much as it did me, because for several minutes they did not speak. They did not look at each other or at me, for which I was grateful. Corn flew by in the headlights.

"If you ever touch me again," my mother finally said, "I'm going to kill you."

My father laughed once, scoffing at her, and I did not like it. At home they both told me it was late, that I needed my sleep.

In August they fought once or twice a week, when I was in bed. I heard my mother come up from watching TV and then an exchange as she walked past my father to the kitchen. I dialed the volume down on my radio, tried to breathe quietly, but they knew I was listening, and instead of going at it in the kitchen, they stopped as if a timeout had been called and moved their argument to the basement. I waited for my father to return, clumping up the stairs, and then the inevitable clatter of the screen door opening as he stalked out. By then Carlsen's corn was better than man-sized. My father walked the rutted tractor path around the field, smoking cigarettes. I'd see him out my window, blending in with the rows, a bright dot easily eclipsed.

Now, late October, they no longer fought. My father walked, my mother watched TV, and I lay in bed. Deep in the night the house was quiet; my father no longer crossed the hall. Mornings we ate breakfast together, overly polite, resigned. I stood outside at the end of our drive hoping my bus would come. We seemed to be waiting for something, saving our energy.

I expected the last night would be the same. In bed I listened to my father zipping up his duffel bag, clapping shut the latches of his suitcase. Long after the spooky theme music closed the show, I lay there waiting for my mother to come up, but when she did, it was not to cry or scream or plead with him but to put away the laundry she'd just done.

"I've got socks of yours," she said.

He thanked her and moved to the bathroom and went through the medicine cabinet.

My mother opened my door, saw that I was awake and told me to go to sleep. "Tomorrow's going to be long," she said. She wrestled with my dresser until her basket was empty, told me to go to sleep again and left.

I followed her footsteps to the top of the basement stairs, where she tossed the basket down and turned out the light. From the living room my father said something to her. She went in to answer him and then, surprising me, sat on the couch. I could not make out what they were saying. All day I had been thinking that tonight was going to be something big, and this was the last chance. I half wanted them to attack each other, throw a lamp through the picture window so the cops would come. Instead, all I heard was mumbling. I crept out of bed to my door and leaned an ear against the bright keyhole.

"I know you can't afford to," my mother was saying. "I'm not saying it's right or wrong, just that you can't afford to."

"I want to," my father said. "I think it's important for him."

"I do too, but you know as well as I do that that's not going to happen. It's all right."

"It's not all right," my father said.

"Well, that's the way it's going to be."

"Where are you going to go?"

"I don't know yet," my mother said. "Somewhere close, somewhere affordable."

I had not heard them talk like this, and though what they said was terrifying, how they said it comforted me. I pressed against the cold keyhole with the same unblinking concentration I fixed on "Radio Mystery Theatre" as they discussed our bank account, our car, living expenses, rent. How deeply my parents felt about these things was a secret to me. It seemed they could not stop talking. My father lit cigarette after cigarette. My mother made them each a drink, then another, and another. My legs were hurting me, so I lay down on the floor. The rush of air under the door made me close my eyes. The ice clinked, my father's lighter scraped up a flame.

"We really did it, Lou," my father said, "didn't we?"

I tried to stay awake, to remember everything they were saying, but it was easily past one and they weren't making a lot of sense anymore. Later I thought I heard them together in the kitchen and—dimly, surfacing for an instant—my mother laughing in the bathroom.

In the middle of the night I woke up not on the floor but back in bed, under my covers. They had not forgotten me, and yet just then I could not allow myself to be grateful to them, for my own sake. I could hear my father snoring, which he did only when he was sick or had been drinking, and I wondered if he had crossed the hall. I put on my nightshirt and opened my door slowly to keep it from creaking. If seen, I would pretend I had to go to the bathroom.

My mother's door was closed, which was normal. The snores were coming from Astrid's room. I stood there defeated in the aqua glow of the nightlight, and then I found that I really did have to pee.

I closed the bathroom door and sat so I wouldn't make so much noise. The seat was cold, and the floor on my feet. I sat in the dark, thinking about tomorrow until my thighs went numb, then gently put down the lid instead of flushing.

My father was still snoring. I thought—melodramatically, because I needed something about this night to be final—that I would never hear him snore like this again. I went to Astrid's door to look in on him, as he had looked in on me so many times.

My mother was in bed with him. The two of them filled Astrid's twin, a trail of clothes on the floor. There were not enough covers, and one of my mother's legs lay cold and exposed, one arm limp as a murder victim's, the wrist delicately bent. I wanted to cover her, to tuck them both in, but didn't dare go near. I leaned in the doorway and wished on them, then went back to my room and got into bed, at last satisfied with the night, hopeful for the morning.

We all slept in late the next day. My father did not have time to shave; my mother ran around the house with the buttons of her uniform undone. At breakfast my father would not sit down. He stood at the counter eating his crumbcake over the sink and writing down emergency numbers for my mother. His bags were already piled by the door in the front hall. My mother insisted on making a hot breakfast for me, and I worked at getting down my runny fried egg and toast. She sat across from me, gulping her cup of coffee.

"I'm not going to have a phone until Monday," my father said. "If you have to get me you can call the super."

"I'll need the furnace man," my mother said. "Did you remember towels?"

He gave her a helpless look and headed for the bathroom.

"Take the blue," she called after him. She took a long draw of coffee, did up her buttons, then looked at me eating. "Do you have practice today?"

"Outside," I said.

"When do I have to come get you?"

"Five," I said. Up until then it had been my father's job to pick me up. So she would have the car, I thought. What else had they decided that I didn't know?

My father passed through with a stack of towels and my mother left her coffee to make her face. I wondered if she was going to drive him to work or whether, like her, he would stand with me at the end of our drive, waiting for someone to pick him up. As I was spooning the gluey dregs of my breakfast down the disposal, a car honked outside. My father opened the screen door and waved, then came back inside.

"My ride's here," he called past me.

My mother came out of the bathroom, tying her hair back so the kids at her work couldn't grab it.

"Arthur," she said, "help your father."

I lifted two small duffels and, elbowing the screen open, followed him out. In our drive idled a weathered white Chevy pickup, at the wheel a dark-haired man I didn't know. Even with his doors closed I could make out the bass line of Steely Dan's "Reelin' in the Years," the closing section Warren and I could do note for note with our mouths. He hopped out to clear a spot in the bed for the bags, and I could see he was wearing the same beige uniform top my father had on. The lozenge above his heart said Glenn, and that was how my father introduced him when we had everything in.

"My boy Arthur," my father said, and Glenn and I shook hands. His hair was short and neat, as if he'd just come out of the Army, and he had a cross on, a big silver one with Jesus in relief, just starting to tarnish. He seemed embarrassed, sorry we were all part of this. He stayed with the truck while my father and I went back inside.

My mother had her coat on now, and was beginning her final sweep, picking up speed as she located her purse, her cigarettes, her keys. Usually my father and I watched her from the table with guarded amusement, but today we waited for her by the door as if she were the one leaving.

"I'll call you tonight when I get settled," my father said.

"That's fine," my mother said, then turned to me and added, "I may be a little late getting you."

"Okay," I said. I grabbed my bookbag and my trombone case from the hall closet, giving my parents the time and privacy to say goodbye.

They did not kiss, as I had envisioned. They just stood there looking at each other.

"I guess this is it," my father said.

"That's your choice," my mother said, and looked at the keys in her hand.

"Lou."

"I can't be late."

"All right," my father said.

He did not shake my hand. We followed my mother out and locked the door behind us. My father got into Glenn's truck; as they zoomed off, he waved, and not knowing what to do, I waved back. My mother got into our car and, looking over her shoulder, backed out onto the road. Pulling away, she looked through her window at me, as if unsure she should leave, like someone who has slowed to pick you up hitchhiking and then at the last second thinks better of it but still feels guilty.

I watched our car dwindle, headed off past the Van Dorns'. It was warm for so late in October; you could smell the ground. The unharvested second-growth corn across the road was high and rustled in the wind, inscrutable. Behind me loomed our house, quiet and empty now. I had a key and thought of going back inside and watching game shows all day like I was sick, but my mother was going to pick me up after practice. I put my trombone case down, hung the strap of my bookbag over our mailbox and stood at the end of our drive and, like every day, waited.

A week before Halloween the realtor came up with someone who would rent our house while it was on the market. It was money, my father said; my mother agreed. That Saturday she started boxing everything except the dishes and the TV. We did not have to be out of the house until mid-November, but she'd found a place we could move into the first, a townhouse apartment in a complex a few miles from us. She was excited when she told me, as if we'd gotten lucky. She wanted me to ride over with her and see it. I knew I would not like the place because I knew from my bus route exactly where and what it was, but to please her

I hopped in the car and while we were there I smiled and acted enthusiastic.

It was not a house and not really an apartment either. Since we only needed two rooms, my mother had rented the top half of a duplex in what had once been the dormitories of a failed seminary school. Foxwood, it was called. The building site had been designed for privacy and meditation; a gravel drive too steep for the bus to navigate in winter disappeared into the woods only to resurface a mile down the road. The developers had kept the name and leveled the chapel. The rubble lay where it had fallen, marked off with stakes painted hunter orange. My mother said the diocese didn't have enough money to keep it running, but the rumors around school involved—predictably—dungeons, orgies and human sacrifice. It was cheap, just a step up from a trailer court. Cars sat up on blocks; muddy toys lay scattered in the grass. Only two girls in my grade came from there—the Raybern sisters, twins—and though they were impeccably neat, they wore homemade calf-length skirts, pleated button-down blouses and belted cardigans as if they were already spinsters. If they had been smart we would have understood them, but they were C students, and therefore weird for no real reason. They sat together near the front of the bus, bony and silent. In the morning when we were nearing the gate, someone in back would call, "Next stop: Fuckwood," and when the Raybern sisters got on we would all be laughing.

When I told Warren, he said "That blows" to make me feel better.

"Don't let her throw any of my shit away," Astrid threatened me from Tennstaedt.

I said I'd try, but it was a hollow promise. Our mother had started with Astrid's room. By the time we talked, she'd already taken a full wagonload of garbage bags down to the Goodwill box in the Foodland parking lot and come back flushed and triumphant. All she had saved were two photo albums, a shoebox of letters and some sweaters she'd tried on to see if they still fit anyone. What I salvaged had been accidental, things I'd stolen over the years and now considered mine—the cooler of her books (Tolkien, Vonnegut, Hunter S. Thompson), her stash with its sweet meerschaum and strawberry-flavored papers and resincoated bowls. Now I'd have to give them back.

Room by room the house emptied out. Every day my mother came home from work and put a pot of coffee on, changed into jeans and a sweatshirt and picked up where she'd left off boxing the night before. The strapping tape came off the roll with a ripping sound; her footsteps echoed. I did not like being in the house with her, and when I did not have band practice I made sure I could put in a few hours at my job, doing food prep and policing the kitchen at the Burger Hut II near school. As the light outside dimmed and the din- ner crowd seeped in, I dredged the dark lake of the Fry-o-lator, imagining myself waiting for the bus with the Raybern sisters.

At home my mother didn't have time to cook and we ate frozen food, rinsing the silver, partitioned trays so her kids at work could paint with them. Without my father at the table, I noticed she talked about the children at her work a lot. "We had one die today," she'd say, or, "Do you remember Monte? He's finally going home." They seemed to me another family she belonged to which I would never share, and I won- dered who she talked to this way about me. We had not started going to Dr. Brady yet; we were still trying to talk to each other.

My father called and dropped by some nights to pack up the garage with all his tools. He was living in a townhouse apartment in a different complex called Lake Vue near the state park. He laughed and joked while we cleaned his wrenches in turpentine and tracked down his missing drill bits, but he was sub- dued around my mother and would not argue with her. He was agreeable to everything she said, and helped with the move even more than he would have normally. He rented the truck when the U-Haul place wanted a credit card and my mother didn't have one, and when we took a load of furniture over to his place (the rec room couch spotted with my mother's burn holes, the wicker peacock throne, the fake deco end tables), he let her drive, following behind in the Country Squire.

Halloween, Warren and I had planned on going to a dance in town. It was just an excuse to get a ride in from his mother so we could egg windows and soap cars. Upholding tradition, my mother had filled a big salad bowl with Clark bars. She knew no one would come and had already begun eating them, washing them down with scotch. She was sitting tailorseat on the living room floor with my transistor tuned to the scratchy classical station from Pittsburgh. We'd finished packing the truck that afternoon. Beside her lay our sleeping bags and a pillow each, our clothes for tomorrow folded neatly in piles. I told her I didn't absolutely have to go.

"Please," she said. "I don't want you moping around here all night. Just don't get into any trouble."

"I won't," I said.

"Don't," she said.

"I *won't*."

We looked at each other, standing by our answers.

"Do you know why we're doing this?" she asked me, and pointed around to the bare walls.

"Because we don't have enough money without Dad," I said, trying my best.

"Because your father won't forgive me for something I did."

I did not, at that moment, want to know what that something was. I wanted Warren's mother to pull into the driveway and honk her horn for me.

"I don't expect you to understand any of this," my mother said, "but I think you should know this isn't my doing or your father's doing but both of our doing. I know what we're doing to you and your sister isn't right, but this is what we've both decided to do." She took a sip of scotch and gritted her teeth, lit a cigarette and blew a quick jet of smoke. "I was in love with a man. Your father can't forgive me that—not that he's perfect on that score. He's seeing someone and has been for some time. Don't think I'm the only villain in this."

"You're not a villain," I said, but dazed, the way a fighter being clubbed against the ropes paws blindly, hoping to tie up his opponent.

My mother put up both her hands for me to be quiet.

"I was in love with a man who didn't even like me.

Isn't that sad? At least some of the women your father loved loved him back. I was in love by myself. It was stupid. There was nothing I could do one way or the other.'' She took a bite of her Clark bar. Standing above her, I could see the waxy white line of her part and the gray mixed into her dark roots. She sniffled and cleared her throat. Much too late, the Hardestys' Bonneville turned into our drive, the headlights floating ghostly across the ceiling. ''Have you heard enough?''

''I guess,'' I said.

''You guess.''

''Yes,'' I said.

''Don't ever become a woman,'' my mother said. She stood up shakily and embraced me. She wasn't crying, she just smelled drunk. ''Promise me.''

''I won't,'' I said.

''Good,'' she said. ''Now go get stoned with your little friend what's-his-name and don't break any windows.''

Mrs. Hardesty let us off in front of Emily Britain— the school that had sponsored the dance—and we walked through the masked, clutching couples and out the fire door into the pleasing anonymity of the dark.

''Let's break shit,'' I said.

''Fuckin A,'' Warren said.

The next morning my father came over driving my

Aunt Ida's clunky old Nova. It was a salt-rotted '65 that sat on its rear axle like a crippled dog. In our garage my father had once refurbished a Triumph TR3 which he later sold to help pay for Astrid's braces, and to see him in my aunt's rattletrap was a shock, as if he too were falling apart.

"It's mine now," he admitted.

"You can't be serious," my mother said.

"I needed something and she wanted to get rid of it."

"Don't blame this on me," she said.

"I'm not," he said. "It'll fix up. It'll be a perfect car for winter. I'll get something in spring. It's not like I'm going anywhere."

"That's true," my mother said.

We did a final reconnaissance of the house, discovering a thermometer stuck by a suction cup to the kitchen window and a plunger for the downstairs toilet that my mother said we could leave. It was a sunny day and the light cut the bare rooms into pieces.

"It looks good," my father said at the door, but my mother didn't let him linger. She closed and locked it and let the screen spank shut.

"Arthur," she said, "can you direct your father?"

It did not take long. We had everything we could fit into the apartment in by noon. The few pieces that didn't make it—the kitchen ensemble, two overstuffed chairs from the rec room, Astrid's bed and desk—we dropped off at a U-Store, my mother draping them with old sheets as if the tiny tin cube were a disused room of a mansion. We made sure we had the key, then rolled down the corrugated door.

Beyond a few children staring at us as my father took off, our neighbors were not interested in us. The super, an older woman in a hunting jacket with a quilted shoulder, came by around five to see if everything was all right. For dinner my mother ordered pizza, which she said we really couldn't afford to do anymore.

"Here we are," she toasted with her free Coke.

"To Foxwood," I said.

We drank, but afterward my mother stared into the greasy box too long. She saw that I'd caught her and smiled.

"It doesn't seem real yet," she said. "It feels like a motel, like we're on vacation. I keep thinking we're going to go home."

"So do I," I said.

"But we're not," she said, trying to be cheery for me. "We're here. This is it."

"I don't mind it."

"Of course you do," my mother said. "Don't be an idiot."

Monday I waited with the Raybern sisters, kicking

at the gravel. They introduced themselves by saying, "You're new." We had been in the same grade for a full year yet they didn't seem to recognize me, let alone know my name.

"Where are you from?" one of them said—Lila, I think. She had cat's-eye glasses and a narrow jaw; her teeth were surprisingly perfect.

"I'm from here," I said. "I've lived here my entire life."

"Not here here," said the other one, Lily. She had the same glasses and big eyes and teeth, but her slump was worse, making her look shorter.

"Butler here," I said. "I'm in Mrs. Reese's homeroom."

We stood there as the wind pushed the birches, making them creak and tilt like masts. Though it was only a mile from our house, the land seemed wild and foreign, a place I might get lost in.

"Oh, Mrs. Reese," Lila said, suddenly brightening. "I know Mrs. Reese."

"Is she the one with the leg?" Lily asked, thinking of Mr. Donnelly, who had a prosthetic foot.

"No," Lila said, "she's the one with the face," which, while accurate, was cruel. Mrs. Reese had had a stroke and the right side of her face was paralyzed.

"What time," I asked, "does the bus usually get here?"

"Late," they both said.

When I got on, the whole bus was laughing.

I don't remember much of the day. Warren and I probably got stoned and cut study hall; Monday morning was a good time to hang around by Marsden's Pond because only the diehards were out. I ate lunch in the cafeteria—a grilled cheese, corn, a block of Jell-O and two chocolate milks for sixty-five cents. In the afternoon I had music, which I never missed, and then it was time to go home again.

I sat in back by the emergency door with Warren and the rest of my friends. The Raybern sisters were up front on the right side, Lila on the aisle. Warren was recounting the plot of last night's "Banacek," a football player disappearing from under a pileup. We were all trying to figure out how they'd pulled off the stunt when the driver, Mr. Millhauser, stopped in front of what was now my old house. He reached out and yanked the handle and the door squeaked open.

Instinctively I reached for my case and my bookbag, then remembered. I suppose no one had told him. Our name was still on the mailbox; there was even a *Pennysaver* lying in the drive.

"Arthur?" Mr. Millhauser said, looking up at his mirror.

My friends—all except Warren—looked to me to see what was up. The other kids in the bus were either whispering or completely quiet. Some were from Lake Vue. I wondered how many knew, and how many right now were guessing. I thought maybe I should just get out and pretend I was going in and then, when the bus was gone, hitch a ride or walk cross-country to Foxwood.

"Arthur Parkinson?" Mr. Millhauser called.

I looked at the dried swipes of mud under the seat in front of me, the bolts holding it to the floor.

"He doesn't live there anymore," Warren said, loud enough for everyone to hear. "He's got a new place."

"Arthur?" Mr. Millhauser asked, as if this might be a joke.

I looked up, ready to tell him the truth, but when I tried to speak my voice caught in my throat. I could only nod. In front, Lila Raybern leaned across the aisle and, hiding her mouth behind a hand, said something to Mr. Millhauser. He closed the door and drove.

F O U R

AT THE LAST MINUTE Annie chooses the new Burger Hut up by the high school. It's cheap, none of her friends work there, and it saves her the trip into town. When she calls—from her mother's, since this is for her benefit—Glenn offers to drive them. He can get his father's car if she doesn't like the truck.

Why don't they meet there, she says, it'll be easier. She doesn't expect any trouble, but if something goes wrong she wants to be able to leave.

"Is that what you're wearing?" her mother asks, meaning her jeans, her black leather jacket hanging in the hall.

"It's the Burger Hut, Ma."

"I'm sure Glenn will have on something nice."

"It's not a date," Annie says. "It's just lunch."

"He's trying. Doesn't that mean anything to you? I'd think you'd be happy for him."

"So he has a job. I have a job *and* I take care of Tara."

"I've heard all of this before," her mother says. She takes a loaf of white from the tin on the counter and starts making a salami sandwich for Tara.

"I don't want to get your hopes up," Annie says. "Or mine."

"Just be nice this once."

"I'm always nice," Annie says. "That's my problem."

Her mother calls Tara in to eat, lays the plate on the table and sits down. Tara lifts the top slice to see what's inside—just mayo, her mother knows how she likes it.

"He is trying."

"Will you stop?" Annie says.

Watching Tara is making her hungry. She takes her purse upstairs and checks her face in the bathroom mirror. She looks tired from working last night, puffy. She finds a jar of Noxzema and runs some water, towels off and goes through her makeup case. In the mirror she draws her eyes on, grits her teeth to see how white. It'll do. She tries on two pairs of earrings, decides against them and brushes her hair. She pulls it back with both hands, a rubber band at the ready between her teeth, then lets it fall and spread. Glenn likes it long. Selfishly, she thinks she needs to get it cut.

Downstairs May notices Annie's new face, secretly pleased. As much as Annie complains, she hasn't been the same without Glenn; everyone says so.

As she's getting ready to leave, Tara starts squalling at the table. "I want to see Daddy, I want to see Daddy." She kicks and cries, making waves in her milk. Annie tries to calm her, though they both know it won't do any good. Tara is screaming now, her face purple, and when Annie reaches for a napkin to wipe her nose, the cuff of her jacket catches Tara's glass and tips it over. The milk pours onto Tara's lap, spatters the chair, Annie's cowboy boots, the floor.

"You little shit," Annie hisses, and grabs Tara by

the shoulders. She swings Tara out of the chair and stands her against the oven, banging her head on the handle. May wants to stop her but, stunned, can't move. She's never ready for Annie's temper; it reminds her of Charles that one time, lunging across the table to get Dennis. But Charles had a reason and Dennis was grown, though like Tara he didn't dare strike back, did not even defend himself. The milk drips. Tara wails, choking on her sobs. "Cut it out," Annie hollers, squatting to look her in the eye, and when she doesn't, smacks her on the bottom. "What is your problem? Why are you giving me such a hard time?"

"It's all right," May says, blotting the mess. Her face is hot, as if she's the one being yelled at, and because she has let this happen, she does feel guilty. Charles never hit her. "You go. I can handle Tara."

"I want you to apologize," Annie demands, but Tara can't stop crying. "God damn you."

"It's just a spill," May says.

"It's just a spill," Annie mimics. "Every day it's a spill. My whole life is a fucking spill."

May comes around the table, trying to calm her down. "It was an accident."

"It's always an accident," Annie says, hard, and looks at May as if daring her to hit her. May had been about to touch her on the shoulder, but her hand stops in midair between them. Annie turns and stalks out of the room and out of the house, leaving the front door wide open, the cold reaching May and Tara in the kitchen.

"It's all right," May says. "Mommy's not angry at you."

Still standing against the oven, Tara heaves and gulps. May gathers her into her skirt. "It's all right," she says. "We'll have some lunch and we'll feel better." She gets her into her booster seat and waits until she's eating again to close the front door. When she comes back, Tara's eyes are red but she's driving her sandwich around the edge of her plate like a train.

"Woo-woo," she says.

"Woo-woo you," May says. "Eat your lunch."

Glenn gets there early, in his Sunday clothes except no tie. He's arranged to take the day off even though he's only begun his thirty-day probation. He's been in this Burger Hut before, but years ago, when it was a Winky's. To him, the real Burger Hut is downtown, across from the parking lot where everyone still hangs out. He and Annie used to end up there after a movie at the Penn. It has a counter and a grill and you have to elbow your way through. This one's typical fast food, a row of swabbed yellow tables like gym equipment between the window booths. The one he sits down at has salt all over it. He takes a napkin and scatters it, makes sure her seat is clean. The place is relatively empty. Pairs of women have drifted over from the shopping plaza, a couple clumps of kids from the high school, a fat man in a suit and tie having two coffees with his meal. Outside a yellow Midas truck grinds by. Glenn checks his watch and looks at the draft from the traffic keeping leaves afloat over the road. His father's Fury sits in the lot, newly washed this morning, and he wonders if Bomber has enough water. His mother says he's crazy if he thinks Annie's going to take him back. His father understands that he has to at least try.

She's late—only ten minutes, but he's sensitive. She doesn't take the empty space on either side of the Fury, instead swings into a spot against the window, the Maverick's front tires hitting the concrete stop, rocking the car back. She gets out and slings her purse over her shoulder and heads purposefully across the lot, then sees the door and angrily reverses direction. By her stride, Glenn can tell she's pissed off. He's not ready for this, but stands to welcome her, unconsciously brushing at his jacket. She opens the door and scans the crowd with the same impatience. He's over-dressed—again—and curses first his luck and then his stupidity. He waves and she sees him.

She doesn't offer her cheek, doesn't even sit down.

"Tough day," he asks.

"Your daughter," she says. "And my mother on top of her. I don't want to talk about it. Did you order yet?"

"I was waiting. What do you want, your usual?"

"Sure," she says, dropping her purse on the seat and taking off her jacket. "Vanilla shake though. My face has to be good for work."

He heads for the counter, hoping she won't call him back to give him money.

At the table Annie lights up and pulls a silvered-paper ashtray in front of her. On the way over she zipped into a Stop-n-Go for a fresh hardpack of Marlboros and had one in the lot with the car off, torturing herself for hitting Tara. She hates losing control like that, but she gets worked up and Tara won't listen. "Do you think I like to yell at you?" Annie screams. She wonders how much Tara understands, how much she'll remember. Annie can't reach that far back, only to first grade, her classmate Vanessa Cheeks standing in the middle of the room, reddening as she pees on the floor.

It's cold next to the window, and she drapes her jacket over her shoulders. She looks around; there's no one who knows them. She doesn't know what she wants from this lunch, why she's here. She's tired of her life being fucked up.

Glenn comes back with the shake and a numbered pickup slip. "I thought you quit."

"I'm just upset."

"What was the trouble?"

"She wanted to come too. Actually she wanted you."

"I know how that can get," he says. "She does that with me all the time. 'I want Mommy, I want Mommy.' It's normal according to my mother."

"Yeah," Annie says. She's heard enough of Olive's wisdom; she doesn't need advice from a woman who's never given birth. She puts out her cigarette and starts on her shake, hoping he'll let it go.

"You're still mad at her."

"More at myself. You know how I am. I get frustrated and lose it."

"When she gets like that there's nothing you can do."

"And my mother acts like it's all my fault."

"Like she never yelled at you," Glenn jokes.

"You know what," Annie says, "I really don't think she did."

"That's ridiculous. That's what parents do, yell at their kids."

"You don't yell at Tara half as much as I do. You're her fun daddy, and I'm mean mommy."

"Only because I'm not home anymore."

"Even when you were there you never yelled at her. You left that up to me."

"You're right," he admits. "You're better at it."

"Thank you," Annie says. "That makes me feel a lot better."

"I didn't mean it that way."

"I know," she says, "I was just kidding."

A speaker over the counter blurts a number she can't make out.

"That's us," Glenn says, and goes up. Annie watches him, thin in his good slacks, and wonders what kind of drugs he's on. He's so calm. She knows he's in treatment for his depression. When she heard he'd tried to kill himself, she didn't exactly feel guilty but unobservant. All winter he'd been on the couch. She'd come home from work and he'd be lying there in the dark with the lights out and a bottle on the floor. He'd say crazy things like "Did you ever think you were Jesus?" Maybe he needed the church all along. It's just sudden, his belief. She's seen this sort of thing fall apart on him before. Still, he seems so sure. Annie doesn't want to admit her mother is right, but he really seems to have cleaned himself up.

When he comes back with the tray, she asks, "You're working."

"At the junkyard. It's a nothing job but the money's good. Actually I like it. I was going crazy staying home."

The word "crazy" makes Annie flush and she takes a bite of fries. There's just one bag; they're sharing.

"I'm going to move out as soon as I get enough money."

"Where would you go?" Annie asks, ready to deflect the wrong answer.

"In town. I don't know."

The burgers are hot and just as good as the real Burger Hut. Hers is medium, the outside charred, just how she likes it; he's remembered that she loves onion and hates tomato. Eating, she notices that he's looking around like she is, checking everyone out as if they're spies.

"I feel like we're onstage," he says.

"Like they all know our business."

"Exactly," Glenn says.

Annie hasn't felt this comfortable with him since they split. She wonders if she should be honest and tell him about Brock, tell him not to get his hopes up, though she knows she won't. There's no reason. They eat, neither of them taking the last fry.

"So," Glenn asks after they've balled up the wrappers and jammed them in the cups, "how are you doing?"

"Okay," she says. "You know. Work, Tara."

"Would you like to maybe see a movie with me next week?"

"I'm probably on."

"Your mom says you have Thursdays off."

"Not always," Annie says, damning her. "I'll have to check my schedule."

"Or do you just not want to go with me? I'd understand."

"It's not that. It's complicated."

"Are you seeing someone else?"

"No," she says automatically. "It's just strange being asked out on a date by your husband. After everything."

Glenn sees he's beaten and slides the tray to the edge of the table. He gets up. "Well, think about it."

"No," she says, "I'll go. If I'm off."

"Great," he says, "okay," and stands there with the tray, dizzied by his luck. He remembers he's supposed to throw the garbage away and locates a can, fits the tray into a stack on top. When he comes back to the table she's pushing her arms through her sleeves, getting ready to leave.

"Here," she says, and gives him three ones. "The whole thing only cost two-fifty."

"You can pay for the movie," she says.

He holds the door for her, looks back into the Burger Hut to see if the crowd is still watching. In a booth opposite he recognizes Don Parkinson's kid. Glenn can't remember his name. He waves. The kid looks straight through him, turns his face away and digs into his burger.

It puzzles Glenn but it's not going to ruin his mood. He catches up with Annie at the Maverick. He doesn't screw things up by pressing for a kiss, just thanks her for coming, says she didn't need to pay.

"What are we seeing on Thursday?" Annie asks.

"Anything you want."

"You pick," she says. "Those are my conditions. And please, wear jeans."

In his father's car Glenn goes over the date—her anger, the vanilla shake, how she said yes while he was holding the tray—follows it beginning to end between exits until he knows it like a favorite song.

Sunday they see each other when Glenn picks up Tara. He brings a huge stuffed bunny Annie thinks is too expensive, meaning she can't afford it. When they first separated, Glenn sent her a check every month, but during his problems he stopped. Unbeknownst to him, his father offered her money, which she indignantly refused. She's a month behind on the rent; luckily the Petersons—her landlords, since they convinced old Mrs. Peterson to leave—are in Florida. She can stall them indefinitely, but Christmas will be coming up before long. A month and a half, and Annie hasn't started shopping. Saturday mornings Tara sits on the couch eating dry cereal and after every talking doll and remote-controlled car commercial points and announces, "I want that."

Tara won't let go of the rabbit. "Bun-bun," she croons to it, and how can Annie take it away? Besides, everything's been going so well. She doesn't want to fight anyone right now. She remembers her father on Easter helping her fill her basket in the backyard. He carried her on his shoulders and outraced her brothers to the next egg. The gift's not malicious, Annie thinks now: Glenn's a father and Tara's his daughter. Yet it's still annoying. She recognizes his helplessness but doesn't understand it. A mother, she can't imagine being so in love that she'd be unable to say no to someone.

When Glenn asks, Annie says yes, she's free Thursday. She can see he's excited, almost as happy as her mother was. "Oh honey," her mother said, hugging her, "that's so good," and Annie had to calm her down. Annie's not sure if she should be excited herself, if this is a step in the right direction. She thinks how bad last winter was, this spring; she still hasn't fully recovered. But she does need help with Tara, and the money would come in handy. He's good around the house.

It's too cold for the lake, Glenn says. He's thinking about the new Aquazoo in Pittsburgh and wonders if Tara is too young. Annie wishes he would stop calling on her to make his decisions, but says sure, she'll get a kick out of it. She waits until they're gone a good fifteen minutes before taking a shower and changing into something Brock hasn't seen.

She takes the back way through Renfrew and gets to Susan's early, before Brock. The lot is half-full; the Steelers are playing the Raiders late. Annie doesn't want to go into the office. The reservation is probably under a fake name anyway. She sits in the car with the motor off and the radio on until she begins to worry about the battery. A low, rent sky slides above the TV antennae. Brock has never been late before, or she's never been early. A heavy man in a green mackinaw and a Kenworth cap slips into Room 6, followed ten minutes later by another man she swears she's seen at the country club. The keys are sweaty in her hand. Beside the office stands a blue phone booth.

She knows the number by heart, having called Barb nightly through her hard times. Annie crouches down in the booth, hoping no one can see her. It's like a mystery on TV, the sniper and the dangling receiver. She hopes he isn't sick.

"Hello," Barb answers sharply.

"Barb," Annie says, improvising. Barb's supposed to be doing brunch at the club; yesterday she double-checked the roster. "Good. I tried you at work."

"Annie," Barb says with an edge that shocks her heart, makes her face flush. "I don't think I want to talk to you right now. Right now I'm talking with Brock. I will talk to you because I have some things I need to say to you but I can't do that right now."

Annie stands in the booth, the protective metal cord cold on her arm. She doesn't want to believe this news. She's never thought this far ahead.

"Barb, I'm sorry."

"I don't care whether you're sorry or not. I don't care what you say to me anymore." She hangs up, leaving Annie staring at the parking lot, her car mixed in with the others before the blank, ugly face of the motel.

"Fuck," Annie says, still holding the phone. She leans her forehead against the dial and shuts her eyes. "Fuck, fuck, fuck."

———

When she gets home Brock's Charger is in the drive. Brock is sitting tailorseat on the hood, staring at the beer in his lap. He has a fresh scratch on his forehead, another on his jaw. The backseat is piled with clothes, albums, a stereo. She thinks of all the stuff Glenn left behind, the dusty boxes in the basement.

"I hope you don't think you're going to stay here," Annie says.

"I don't have anywhere else to go." At least he's not drunk, Annie thinks, just crushed. She wonders if he loved Barb after all, but is too scattered herself to feel sorry for him.

"What about your aunt's?"

"She doesn't want to see me."

"I can't," Annie says.

"A week. Just until I get a place. I'll pay rent, I'll do the dishes. One week, I promise."

"What time is it?" Annie asks, and looks at her own watch. "Come in and we'll talk. Leave the stuff here."

Inside she gets a beer. He's forgotten his, and paces, and she makes him sit. They take opposite ends of the couch, as if they're breaking up. Brock hasn't kissed her yet, and won't.

"What happened?" Annie asks.

"It was stupid. She found a carbon from the motel

in the wash. It was all balled up but she could read it. She popped it on me and I didn't know what to say."

"So you told her it was me."

"I couldn't lie to her."

"What do you mean?" Annie says. "You've been lying to her for weeks."

"She knew," Brock says. "You were the first name she came up with."

"And you said yes."

"What was I supposed to say?"

"That's great," Annie says. Like a dog on a chain, her mind keeps leaping after possibilities only to choke on the fact that Barb knows. "Well, there's nothing we can do about it now. Listen, Glenn's going to be here in twenty minutes. Why don't you go buy us some dinner and come back around six. I don't want him seeing you here."

"What kind of food do you want?"

"I don't care," Annie says. "Something Tara can eat."

"Like what?"

"Fish, chicken, anything. Just get out of here."

"Annie," Brock says.

"Don't start," Annie says, and then it's her turn to pace.

Friday night when Glenn's mother tells him there's a man living at Annie's he doesn't believe her. He was there Sunday. Annie had to cancel their date yesterday to cover for another girl at work, but she rescheduled it for next week when she'll be on days. His mother says she's just trying to save him trouble later. Clare Hardesty's seen the fellow's car going in and out of there. Glenn doesn't understand why she constantly has to tear his hopes down. They get into it in the kitchen, and Glenn's father comes in rattling the *Eagle*.

"Why don't you give her a call?" he suggests.

"Better," his mother says, "take a drive over and see for yourself."

Glenn calls and gets Annie. The girl she spelled last night is trading the favor. Annie laughs at the accusation.

"She's probably seeing my mother's car. I'm trying to get her out of the house more."

Glenn lets it go, doesn't say that Clare knows the Polara (she has a Dodge herself, an ugly little Dart). He tries to remember when she's lied to him before and can't. Up until this, everything has been his fault.

Annie reminds him of their date Thursday, says she'll see him on Sunday.

"So?" his mother says when he gets off.

"It's her mother's car."

His mother scoffs, blowing out a mouthful of air.

"Livvie," his father says.

"I've tried," she says. "No one can say I haven't tried."

Glenn wants to hurt her, to say to her face that she doesn't love him, that she's not his real mother, but doesn't. His father gives him a pitying look (he's always sorry, always trying to help him because he's such a fuck-up), and as he has so often since he's been home, Glenn turns and takes his jacket from the back door and leaves them without a word.

Not knowing who it is, Bomber snarls, then recognizes Glenn. The spotlight at the corner of the porch goes on—his father again—and the oak's bare branches throw shadows over his truck. Bomber hears his keys and wants to go with him. Glenn lets him off the chain and the dog goes straight for the driver's-side door.

On the way through town he stops at the 7-Eleven for a six of Iron City. He needs to talk to Rafe, an old high school buddy he used to work with when he was still with Annie. He lives out past the middle school in the house his parents left him. The furniture is ash and cherry, the rugs frayed bare. When Glenn needed a place, Rafe was willing to give him a room. It didn't last long, they were both too screwed up and lost their jobs. They would talk, nodding drunk, late at night when they knew they had to get up for work, of how Tara was the only thing Glenn had ever done right in his life. Rafe is sterile. He'd hold Glenn and sob, trying to explain himself. "You've got Tara, man, no matter what happens, you've got her, man."

"Come on, man," Glenn said, "don't start this shit again."

"You're right," Rafe would say, sniffling, trying to laugh. "You know I can't help it."

But now when Glenn turns into the muddy drive he sees Rafe's place is dark except for a chore light over the garage. His Bronco's gone. Bomber paws the window, thinking they're going to get out.

"Take it easy," Glenn scolds him. He cracks an Iron, slaps the magnetized opener back against the dash, but it falls into Bomber's footwell. "My fucking day."

He drives out to the lake and sits at a picnic table. Across the water the lights of summer cottages describe the shoreline. In the wind the beer feels warm. The swings creak. Bomber runs in and out of the dark, a blur. Glenn wonders what Nan would recommend. It's been too cold, November; he hasn't seen her in weeks. He has her number somewhere, and he can always look in the book.

The stars are up. He leans back against the table to watch them. Sometimes in church he thinks of Jesus stepping down out of the sky, pulling the night aside like a curtain and showing Glenn his blazing flesh, trailing the sword of judgment. Glenn has decided he is not saved yet, that Jesus sees his sin for what it is. When he kneels and closes his eyes for the Confession, he sees his father's watery face, feels the scrape of the hose down his throat, the suction plunging his stomach. None of that has changed, he thinks. He can see himself doing it every day, every time he sees the aspirin hidden away from him in the downstairs bathroom medicine cabinet. "And deliver us," he prays, "from evil. For Thine is the kingdom and the power and the glory. Forever and ever. Amen."

He thinks of his real father's childhood beneath the lake, the dust of a small town summer. "Bullshit," he says, and sees his mother drunk in the Pittsburgh bus station, asking servicemen for quarters. She was the one who put him up for adoption, not his father, but Glenn never blames her. "At least she tried," he says, finds his beer's dead and pops another. He closes his eyes, after a minute opens them. These ghosts won't go away that easily.

The stars retreat and surge forth again; the wind rattles the trees. Glenn finishes the six and dunks the empties thunderously in a raccoon-proof trashcan.

Bomber knows it's time to go and waits for him at the door.

"I'm coming," Glenn says, trudging uphill.

He has no intention of driving by Annie's. Only as the high school exit comes up does he relent, angling the truck up the ramp and braking late for the stop sign. He's not drunk, just buzzed enough to laugh at the giant, spotlit Big Boy in his checked overalls atop the Eat'n'Park. The drive-in bank says it's past midnight and cold enough to snow. He turns left, away from the blue GAS and FOOD arrows, and the lights of town sparkle in Bomber's window.

"That's not where we're from, buddy," Glenn says, and pats him on the shoulder.

The streetlamp halfway down Turkey Hill sheds an empty circle over the road, painting its cracks and potholes black. Beyond it, far off as stars, glow the windows of the Cape. Glenn turns his lights and his motor off and coasts down the slope. He can't see anything until he glides beneath the streetlamp, and then it's too late to turn back.

In the drive sits Annie's Maverick.

"Ha," Glenn says, and shoves Bomber as if they'd bet on it and the dog has lost. He stops and Bomber almost falls into the footwell. They're still a few hundred yards away, out of range in the dark. Above the house the water tower rises swimming pool blue, the tank patched with painted-over names. The woods are dark, the night above them searchlit by the passing traffic on the interstate. Last summer he and Annie took their sleeping bags into the field and with Tara between them watched the stars until the bugs got bad. He thinks he should show up Halloween night in disguise, maybe pin a cape on Bomber.

"What do you think?" he asks. "Superdog, Scooby Doo?"

Bomber cocks his head.

"You pick something then."

Bomber paws his leg. He doesn't know what's going on, why they're stopped so close to home.

"Okay, bud," Glenn says, and starts the truck up. He's hoping Annie's either asleep or watching TV. With his lights off he does a three-point turn that becomes a five-pointer and sneaks up Turkey Hill in first.

At the T across from the Hardestys (asleep, the downstairs dark), Glenn flips on his lights. He has to wait for a car to pass, but the car slows—suddenly, as if the driver thinks Glenn is a cop—and then turns into Turkey Hill, its lights raking the truck, tossing up dust from the berm.

The car passes Glenn, then stops. He recognizes the taillights from work—a '72 Charger—and makes the connection. It's Barb and her boyfriend. The kitchen's closed and they're looking for a party. Glenn doesn't know how he's going to explain his being here and thinks the best way might be to confess right now, to back up and talk to them, say he knocked but no one was home.

He shifts into reverse and looks over his shoulder to see where he's going. The Charger's taillights flare, then return to normal, pulling away.

They've seen him, he thinks. He can't leave.

He does a better three-pointer and heads back toward the house, already testing excuses. The Charger is passing under the streetlamp, moving pretty good. He knows Brock likes to drive.

But it's not Brock, Glenn sees, because the Charger doesn't cut into the drive. It reaches the turn-around, lights shining on the guardrail, and slowly swings onto the dirt road that leads back to Marsden's Pond. It's a make-out place. In the summer they'd hear cars all night, glass smashing, whoops and howls. Every so often the cops would come. Since Glenn's left, Annie has mentioned she has one of her father's old guns if there's any trouble, but there hasn't been. He still worries about her. It's his best and maybe his only reason for being here and, off the hook now and chivalrous with drink, he suddenly believes it's true. He is her protector, whether she appreciates it or not.

He stops before the streetlamp and turns around

again, this time keeping his lights on. If she hasn't seen him yet she's not going to.

At the intersection Glenn takes a left, then makes a U-turn and pulls the truck off to the side, kills the lights. He's hidden by the trees but poking out enough so he can see the turnaround and the house. He wants to see the Charger come out again; he wants to be sure before he tells his mother. Bomber's confused.

It's foolish, he thinks after a few minutes. He has to get up for work tomorrow and he already has a headache from the beers. He's about to give up when he sees a light moving through the woods.

It's the Charger, backing up the dirt road. It comes out under the tower, swings its lights toward Glenn.

"That was fast," he says.

He waits for it to come up Turkey Hill, but it doesn't. It turns into the drive behind the Maverick and someone gets out. Glenn wipes his breath from the glass, and when that doesn't work, jumps out of the truck and runs closer in the cold, shielding his eyes to see better as if it's sunny. At this distance, in the glow from the windows, it could be Barb or Brock or anyone. The driver walks across the lawn. The door opens, and this new light is enough for Glenn to see that the driver is in fact Annie, her hair blazing, so that the taller person beside her, the one taking the bag from her and kissing her, is logically Brock.

Annie hates day shift, especially in winter, but it's the only way she can keep her job. Barb has turned the other girls on nights against her; it's impossible to work. Her time card keeps disappearing, and on the roster someone writes "Sleaze" by every mention of her name. Infuriatingly, Clare Hardesty has said that despite what everyone thinks, she will still sit for her, and when her mother spends the day visiting friends at the Overlook Home (where, ironically, Brock works), Annie reluctantly leaves Tara with Clare, whom she neither likes or can afford. Annie tends the few lunching couples in the main dining room, takes a tray of Manhattans to a table in the bar. By three it's empty. On break she drinks her free Tab and watches the leaves stampede over the deserted golf course. The gay festoons of crepe paper strung for the upcoming Turkey Trot mock her. She ends up prepping for supper, chopping lettuce and decorating relish trays with the dropouts in the kitchen. All they play is classical because Michael the cook likes it, and driving to pick up Tara, she lets WDVE wail—Aerosmith, "Dream On."

"Listen," Glenn says over the phone, "I forgive you."

She hangs up and the phone rings under her hand.

"We are all forgiven. I believe that. I have to believe that."

"Please," she says, "I don't want to have to call the police."

"You're fucking him," Glenn says, "right in our bed. How can you do that?"

Barb calls her once to make it clear that she doesn't mind losing Brock. It's Annie that's hurt her, and she doesn't know why.

"Why did you do it?" Barb asks, after bitching her out, telling her tearfully that she can never be her friend again. Annie can't answer. She thinks of when Barb split with Mark, how she consoled her, the two of them sitting on Barb's fire escape, drinking peppermint schnapps and listening to the PBA teams in the churchyard making the chain nets ring. When they had drained the pint she wrote Mark's name on the foil and made Barb kiss it and throw it into the dumpster below. It smashed and the boys playing ball all looked.

"I don't know. You know how sometimes you do crazy things."

"No," Barb accuses, in one word refuting her argument. "You do what you choose to do."

"Then I don't know," Annie says. "It wasn't him, or if it was it's not anymore. And it wasn't you, I swear to God I didn't want to hurt you."

"But you did."

"I did," Annie says. She's tired of apologizing, and listens to the silence. She can't go any lower.

"Was it worth it?" Barb asks. "Did you get what you wanted?"

"No."

"Glenn called me. He sounded even more fucked-up than usual."

"I know," Annie says. "He's been calling me every day. He's been calling me at work."

"So I hear," Barb says. "You know what I say? I say you deserve whatever you get."

"I can't quit," Annie says.

"That's not my problem," Barb says. "You're a big girl. You did this to yourself. Just don't expect me to talk to you. Stay out of my way."

When they're done, Annie is disappointed, as if she'd expected more. She's surprised Barb called at all. I wouldn't have, she thinks. The whole thing reminds her of high school, how easy it was to give herself to someone for a week, a month, how hard it is now. Trust wasn't what she needed then (and still isn't, she wishes; she's young, it's not her fault she fell in love). She doesn't expect Barb to forgive her immediately.

Her mother's not happy with her either. She says Annie could have told her about Brock, but then won't come over when he's there. Annie knows she thinks she's a fool, that she does these things with no regard for the consequences. Whether it's true or not, Annie thinks her mother should be on her side. They spar where Tara can't hear them.

"Obviously you take after your father," her mother lets slip.

"What is that supposed to mean?" Annie asks.

Her mother ignores her as if she'd never said it. "It's not you I worry about, it's Tara."

"Everything is fine," Annie insists. "There's nothing to worry about."

"Olive called me," she says. Usually Glenn's mother is a joke they share but not now. "It sounds like he's taking it hard. You can't blame him."

"This has nothing to do with Glenn," Annie says, but even she doesn't believe it. She recognized his truck the other night. "He's been calling me," she admits. "Saying things."

"He's hurt. Surely you can see that."

"I'm not afraid of him."

"You know that you can always stay here if you want."

"I have a home," Annie says, tired of having to explain her life. They stop talking, call it a draw.

"Oh honey," her mother says, not satisfied with the tie, "I wish you had told me."

The only saving grace, Annie thinks, is Brock. To think she wanted him gone. His shift at the Overlook Home gets off at eleven. Three afternoons a week he watches Tara. He lets her ride his neck, swings her around by the feet. Watching cartoons, he reads the captions for her—"Acme Rocket Company," "Tasmanius Horribilus"—explains what 4-F was. They stay in their pajamas all day, snuggling under her blanket. Like Glenn, he leaves the discipline to Annie, which is right because Tara's not his daughter. If they were serious it would be different. Sometimes watching him sling her over his shoulders, Annie reconsiders him, thinks that now she can count on him—until he comes home at one in the morning reeking of weed. All she can think of is that he cheated on Barb. He apologizes, says he's not used to living with a family.

"Then you had better get used to it quick," she warns him, but only because she's been working all day and had wanted to spend the few sane hours she has with him. In bed she forgives him, and they sleep folded into each other.

Later that week they're sleeping when Annie wakes to breaking glass, a dog barking far off. It's too close to be coming from the pond. Again, in front. The clock radio says three-fifteen. She jostles Brock.

"I hope that's not him," he says, "because I will kick his fucking ass." He rolls out of bed and lands feet-first as if he's been ready for this. He takes his jeans off the closet doorknob and yanks them on over his pajama bottoms, lets the belt buckle dangle. From outside comes another crash, and across the hall Tara wakes up, complaining. Annie picks up Tara and follows Brock to the head of the stairs. She waits at the top while he goes down to the front door and with a finger lifts the curtain.

"It's him," Brock says, and before she has a chance to react, clicks the outside lights on and opens the door. "Hey!" he shouts. "Fuckhead!"

"Brock!" she whispers, trying to call him back in. She hears Glenn shouting something and rushes into the front room to see what's happening. They keep the door shut to save on heat, and the chill makes her hold Tara closer, stroke her for warmth. She leaves the lights off and goes to the window.

Below, Glenn's truck sits in the middle of the road, Glenn in the headlights, waving his arms, a beer in one hand. He's lumbering drunk, surrounded by smashed bottles. Bomber's in the cab, going nuts. Beyond the truck the field stretches black to the woods; the water tower glows like a blue moon.

"It's Daddy," Tara peeps.

"No, baby," Annie says, "it's someone else."

"Daddy," Tara shrieks, "Daddy."

"Shush," Annie says, "it's not Daddy," and

squeezes her, turns so she can't see. She sways as if Tara's a baby again.

Brock stands in the frosted yard in his pajama top, barefoot, trying to reason with Glenn. Annie thinks of her father's gun in her night table, the telephone by her side of the bed. Tara squirms in her grip, trying to see.

Glenn tosses his beer into the air and lets it shatter at his feet. He points at Brock, shakes his finger at him. Brock shrugs, palms up—what's the trouble?—then waves Glenn toward him with both hands as if helping someone park a car. Glenn steps to the edge of the property; Brock moves toward him, then stops. They lean forward to bellow at each other over an invisible line. Bomber's claws scrabble at the window.

Annie can see the steam coming out of their mouths and hear how loud they're yelling, but the words are lost in Tara's sobs. She thinks that it won't do any good to call the police; they won't get here in time. She carries the struggling Tara into her bedroom and closes the door, goes into her own bedroom and gets the gun.

It's unloaded so Tara can't hurt herself with it, but Glenn won't know that.

"It's okay, honey," she shouts at Tara through the door, and heads downstairs.

Outside, the stoop is freezing on her feet. It's all

over. Brock is sitting on Glenn's chest like in a school-yard fight and shouting into his face, "Don't you ever try to pull shit like this with me again." Bomber has steamed up the cab. Glenn has a cut under his eye and his teeth are rimmed in blood. His upper lip is torn like a thumbed peach. Brock looks fine except his pajama top is ripped. He sees the gun and tells her to put it away. Glenn turns his head and spits out a dark string.

"I'm going to let you up," Brock says. "I want you to get in your truck and get out of here, you understand? I don't want to hurt your dog."

Glenn nods, but at the same time looks at Annie, trying for some sympathy. His eyes swim; she's never seen him so drunk. But his face. It's his fault, she thinks, and turns away.

"Move back," Brock warns her, then says, "Okay, Smokin' Joe," and pushes himself off Glenn.

Glenn rolls over. Wet leaves stick to his back. On his hands and knees he touches his fingers to his mouth and then his cheek. He gets up like an old man, stumbles and makes his way across the yard, not looking back. Annie takes Brock's arm and they watch him fit himself into the truck. Bomber mobs him. It takes him a minute before he shuts the door. He gets it in gear, but before he crunches across the smashed glass, leans out and spits again.

"I will not be deceived by this world," Glenn says in a croak. He's crying.

"Take off, you shithead," Brock says, and gives him the finger.

As the truck passes under the streetlamp, Brock massages his knuckles and spits, puts a finger to his lips. "I think I chipped one of the ones in front." He lifts his chin and smiles for her, and while she's inspecting him, asks through clenched teeth, "Did you call the cops yet?"

F I V E

MY MOTHER INSISTS that the snow never left that winter. According to her, the first flurries struck in mid-November and we didn't see the grass again until spring. I clearly remember a flock of toddlers bulky as astronauts in their snowsuits playing on the moonscape of frozen mud beneath the jungle gym, but the strict truth is unimportant; what my mother is trying to say is that we were cold at Foxwood, which we were.

Our apartment had no thermostat. We found out when two weeks after we moved in the temperature dropped twenty degrees overnight. My mother went from room to room, expecting a box on the wall.

"Arthur," she called, "come help me."

When we couldn't find one, she sagged onto our couch and held her forehead with both hands. "I'm sorry," she said.

"It's okay," I said.

The super said that our building was on a schedule, which meant we heard a feeble clinking in the electric baseboard as we were waking up. The lower halves of the windows were coated with ice. My mother put on coffee and bought a soft toilet seat. We wore sweaters to bed.

By then my mother had decided that moving to Foxwood had been a mistake, but she had signed the lease and we were stuck. She was angry she had been fooled by the new paint and wall-to-wall carpeting. Daily she apologized for the lack of hot water as if it were a crime, then ten minutes later shrieked at me for not unplugging the toaster. She needed my help, she said, didn't I see that?

Mornings I was careful to agree with her first

choice for breakfast. Without my father to serve, we were early. My mother was not used to it. She wandered through the apartment at half speed, trying to find her lighter, her lipstick, her driving gloves. I stuffed the pockets of my jean jacket with matches, Marlboros and whatever I had to share with Warren and buttoned the flaps, hauled on my fat down jacket and gloves and said I was leaving.

"Christ almighty," she said from the other room, and cut short her search to look over my clothes and give me a kiss—something she'd stopped when I was in middle school. She saw my trombone case and, regardless of the day, asked if she needed to pick me up. I merely said yes or no. Outside, a cold surge of relief hit me, and at the same time a feeling of shame at having escaped.

At the bus stop Lila and I talked and shared cigarettes while Lily sniped at us, jealous. "Mom is going to kill you if she finds out."

"So what?" Lila said. Since she'd rescued me, I had begun to wonder what she looked like without her glasses, and was working up the courage to ask her if I could try them on. We had turned our clocks back weeks ago, and a gray half light lingered over the treetops like fog, softening her face. It was hard to flirt with Lily beside her all the time.

From our frigid mornings together, I found that

both Raybern sisters loathed Foxwood as much as I did, for the same reasons. I dreaded getting on the bus to that laughter I used to be part of. I hated being left off at the gate in the snow like a trio of orphans and having to walk half a mile down the drive to reach the smashed chapel and our barrackslike townhouses. When I groused about the landlord—some corporation from Baltimore—Lila and Lily just nodded. It made me like them. I think now that I mistakenly pitied them because I assumed they would never get out, while I was just there temporarily. At school I acknowledged them in the halls, and people looked at me. In a stall on the third floor by my homeroom, someone wrote, "Arty Party Eats Fox Meat."

I only told Warren.

"Lila Raybern?" he said. "Are you shitting me?"

"What's wrong with her?"

"I don't know," Warren said. "She's crazy and has a twin sister. Isn't that enough?"

"She's nice," I said.

"That and she dresses like Mr. Rogers."

"Okay," I said, "I'll give you that one."

In school I could almost pretend my life hadn't changed. I skipped gym and study hall with Warren, then wandered back from Marsden's Pond around lunchtime. It was that in-between season when only the dead trees hold their leaves and the sky threatens constantly. Going inside, stoned, I looked back at the woods as if they were a promise, a haven.

Tuesdays and Wednesdays I practiced in the music room, and Fridays watched snowflakes dissolve on the plastic-coated music attached to my tarnished, dented bell. For homecoming we were doing an all-Sousa revue. In class Mr. Chervenick praised my embouchure and outside hustled up behind me during the tornado, shouting, "That's the way, Arthur, lift those knees!"

My mother was invariably late picking me up. Sometimes I was the last one standing there by the locked doors, and I wondered if she could have forgotten. It was dusk, the dark was falling a little earlier each day; below, in town, the streetlights came on in strings, as if in a humming room somewhere a man was flicking switches. Every few minutes the janitor with his pushbroom and stub of a cigar peered out at me. But no, here she was, just late, apologetic. We rode home past our old house, no longer commenting on it. Instead, she told me about her work and asked after my classes, listed all the tasks she needed to get done. She talked from the time I climbed in until she parked beside the cheesy coachlight in front of our apartment. I liked riding with her even less than the bus. It was here, spinning alongside the cropped fields, that she asked me questions I did not want to answer.

"Do you want me to call your father?"

I watched the gray, see-through barns sail by.

"Do you need to talk to Astrid?"

Beside the road, green signs the size of playing cards told workmen where the lines changed from solid to dotted.

"I don't know what you want me to do."

"Nothing," I said, but she could not accept that this was the truth.

At home, cooking dinner with her shoes off, she badgered me about my unhappiness, my slipping grades, my cigarettes.

"Next year if I can help it we'll be out of here," she said over our Hamburger Helper. She did not know much, she said, about handling money, but she would be careful. We would be all right. While she was used to doing everything for us, I could see it was a strain on her to be so hopeful for me. She did not suddenly become tough and efficient, as I had wished, but put on a false, nearly tireless optimism that I had always associated with my father and that—naturally, as a teenager—I partly believed yet refused to share.

I helped her with the dishes and retreated to my room to practice and then, when the neighbors complained, to listen to my headphones. My mother smoked and watched TV, sometimes having a glass of my father's scotch, never more than two. When her show was over—*Upstairs, Downstairs,* or one of those

112

snooty movies about a weekend-long party at an English country mansion—she would look into my room, carrying an ashtray, and start talking at me as if she'd only been taking a break. Take off the headphones, she gestured, and trapped, I did. We did not discuss what she had done or who my father was seeing; that was in the past. She told me things I didn't want to know about the relatives of her co-workers; she replayed conversations she'd had in her travels around the county. I knew she was lonely but by that time of night I was tired of her using me as an audience. I wanted to fall asleep to *Dark Side of the Moon* and forget everything that had happened to us in the last month, and I resented her for reminding me of it, simply by her presence. I sensed, in her flow of words, a desperation I myself was trying to overcome.

Around the house I tried to fill in for my father where I could. We were still going through boxes from the move, trying out the few different combinations of furniture the tiny living room allowed. I stood around like my father would have, and when my mother pointed, picked up a table or chair or the end of the couch and then stood aside again. It was my job now to take out the trash and lug it to a communal dumpster in the visitors' lot. When my mother asked which dish I would rather have for dinner, I learned to prefer one firmly over the other, when in truth I did not care. But

I could not talk to her the way my father had, I could not argue with her. Even if he did little around the house, when something important came up, we looked to my father to tell us what to do. Right or wrong, in the end he was responsible. When my mother tried to discuss something serious with me—like what we would do about my sister returning from Germany in May, or whether we should break the lease—I had nothing to say to her, gave back only faint echoes. She sighed, letting me know that I was no help, that she would have to decide by herself. And at night I could not replace my father, but lay awake across the hall from her, wishing she wasn't so alone.

One snowy morning at the bus stop, I was talking with Lila when we heard a car spinning its tires on the drive. The high-pitched whine of rubber on ice cut through the trees, and furious bursts of the engine. I knew from the roar that it was our Country Squire. My mother had been meaning to pick up a set of chains. I flicked my cigarette into the snow and, like a hero, coolly excused myself.

I followed our bootprints down the winding drive. It was slippery if you kept to the tracks, but the edges and the hump had a few inches of wet hardpack good for traction. The sound of the engine was coming closer, idling now behind a bend, then suddenly stopped. Beside me in the ditch a trickle made its way downhill. In the woods, snow dropped from the high pines.

It was her. The rear of our car was in the ditch on the right side, the long hood angled out over the road, only one front tire touching the ground. My mother was still inside, and when I jumped the trickle to make sure she was all right I could see she'd been crying but was done now. Her keys were on the dash. She had her driving gloves off and was smoking a fresh cigarette.

"You think they'd salt the goddamn thing," she said.

"What if I push?"

"This car?" She got out and pocketed her keys, put on her winter gloves. "What's the guy's name with the tow truck—the guy with the beard? I'll see if he'll do it for free."

"I know him," I said. "I'll go."

"You've got school," she said, and started walking down the drive. It was a long way but I could not argue, only watch her go. She'd made it twenty feet when she fell, yelping with surprise.

It would have been funny—it was funny—but my mother had had enough. She thrashed around in the snow, screaming, "You son of a bitch, I hate you," kicking and flinging her purse about like a mace.

I scuttled over to her, but by then she had stopped and lay there as if shot, her made-up face in profile against the snow, jaw set.

"Is anything broken?" I asked.

She would not look at me, and I knew better than to push it. I looked skyward at the pines, back at the car.

"Help me up," she said.

That night she called Astrid and hung up and waited with her hand on the phone for my sister to call back. The Air Force gave her a certain number of minutes free a month, and special rates after that. They talked for almost an hour before my mother motioned me over.

"What are you doing?" Astrid demanded.

"What?" I said.

"Are you doing anything at all for Mom?"

"Yes," I said, reasonably, so my mother wouldn't know we were fighting.

"I'm not there, so you've got to help her."

"I am."

"Obviously you're not because she's flipping out. Do you know what time it is here?"

"No," I said.

"It's four in the morning."

"It's been a bad day."

"I guess so," Astrid said. "It's been a bad day for

me and it hasn't even started yet. Will you do something for me?''

"Yes."

"Will you please take care of her until I get back there?''

"I'll try," I said, but again with that sick feeling that accompanies a promise you know will be broken.

Now, more often, I signed up for the last shift at the Burger Hut and after practice walked the exhaust-blackened half mile with my case to punch in and tie on my apron. Weekdays the kitchen closed at nine, and the last hour I was allowed to man the register. It was easy—all the different items were typed right on the buttons and no one talked to me except to ask for ketchup. Closing, I refilled the air deodorizers in the restrooms with pink syrup and dusted the rubber plants. Before punching out, I projected my hours to see how much money I'd keep after giving my mother half. (I was saving for a Stratocaster copy Warren had seen in the pawnshop downtown even though I didn't know how to play guitar.) Mr. Philbin, the manager, gave me a ride home, and as if he knew what awaited me, tuned in the country-western station and said nothing.

But the Burger Hut was not half the respite Friday night became when my mother started going out with friends from her work. After dinner she changed out of her uniform and into one of two spangly cocktail dresses. Red and blue, they were both short and—she thought—tended to make her legs look a touch heavy. Lying on my bed with Jimi Hendrix thundering, I pretended not to watch her ritual in the bathroom across the hall. She leaned into the mirror to dab on eye shadow, tilted her head to fasten her earrings. With her face made, she looked much younger. I had never been forced before to consider whether my mother was attractive, and while I was intimidated by this version of her, I was also relieved that she had friends and that she trusted me to stay home alone.

The minute our car passed the chapel, I went to my room, opened the window and stoked a bowl. I sprayed Ozium just in case, its lemony scent thick as mist. I ransacked the cupboards, then settled for Pepsi and Pop-Tarts and planted myself on the couch to watch TV. Around eleven—as I was worrying when she'd be home—the police from the sheriff's office would show up, their lights strobing in the trees as they eased down the icy drive. Like the Lawsons downstairs from us, I'd slip on my coat and go out in the snow to watch them referee our neighbors' disputes. I don't remember anyone throwing a punch, only a lot of grappling and cursing, the men from the sheriff's office talking to people in their warm front seats. At eleven-thirty "Chiller Theatre" began, which I never missed. My mother came in around one, just as John Carradine was being strangled by his latest creation. She drew a tall glass of tap water and sat down beside me, chain-smoking while I told her the plot.

"Where did you go?" I asked, as if I knew the bars around town. "How was it?"

All week she had been assaulting me with the most insignificant details of other people's lives, but now all she said was, "DJ's. It was okay."

If she was drunk, she'd put her arm around me and say, "You're a good kid, you know that? Jesus, what time is it? I've got to go to bed. You should too." In minutes I'd hear her snoring. I'd look in and make sure the covers were on her, and the next morning let her sleep while I cooked breakfast.

Saturdays my father was supposed to visit, but he hadn't yet. Though my mother talked to him over the phone, we had not seen him since the move. My mother had put together a garbage bag full of his stuff she'd dug out of her bureau drawers. It waited for him on the landing outside our door.

I did want to see him, partly because I missed him and partly because, as I told my mother, he had promised to teach me to drive. I was going to be fifteen in the spring, old enough for my learner's permit. I was signed up for Driver's Ed and already had the manual.

I thought that once I had access to a car I would be besieged by girls. At the least I could take Lila Raybern to the Sky Vue Drive-In.

"That's not what I'm asking," my mother said. "I can teach you how to drive. Do you want to see your father or not?"

"Sure," I said. "Yes."

She called him and put me on, holding the phone out as if daring me to take it. She pointedly left the room.

"Arty," my father said, and asked me how I was holding up. My father is not a talker and neither is his son. I stood closemouthed in the living room, trying to make him fill the silences. We dismissed the Steelers and the snow.

"So," my father said. "I've been meaning to have dinner with you. How's this Saturday?"

"Okay," I said, trying to sound bored.

"Okay," he said. I paced between the couch and TV. "Okay, how about putting your mother back on?"

I dropped the phone on the couch and hollered for her.

Lake Vue, where my father now lived, was new. I had never been in it, but when the bus picked up, the kids who got on there were wearing neat Levi's and rugby shirts and blue suede Puma Clydes. They were semi-preppy in their down vests, and scorned long-hairs like Warren and me. I imagined them poking fun at my aunt's old Nova.

As the week progressed, I grew to resent the Lake Vue kids.

"The lake's not even there," I explained to Lila. "It's a good five miles away. The only view they have is the Agway across the road."

"Yeah," she said, "but I bet they've got hot water."

By the time my father came to pick me up Saturday, I blamed him for leaving us to rot at Foxwood while he and the mystery woman he was seeing blew my and my mother's money at Lake Vue.

He was on time, driving the Nova. The bumper was sticking out of the trunk, the rear quarter-panel crumpled.

My mother came outside in her sweater and made sure I had the bag of his stuff. She didn't want him to come in because the place was messy. The three of us stood on the lower landing in the cold.

"What happened there?" she asked—gleefully, I thought.

"Little fender bender," my father said.

"Little," my mother said.

"It'll fix up." It had been three weeks since we'd seen him. I had expected him to look different, somehow changed or dressed-up, but there he was, my father, in his steel-toed workboots and jeans, unshaven because it was a Saturday. "Have you talked to Astrid?"

"Yes," my mother said.

"How is she?"

"Fine."

My father waited but that was all she was going to give him. "Well, good," he finally said. "Arty, are you all ready?"

"He has some things you left."

My father thanked her and took them, and without peeking in the bag, put it in the backseat. While they hashed out when he would return me, I slid into the front. My mother waved me away as if I were leaving for good.

The Nova made it up the drive easily. Though he owned it, it was not my father's car. The seats smelled of my aunt's cigarettes, and my father had either observed or not disturbed her ritual of keeping a useless box of tissues on the shelf beneath the rear window. We headed west, away from Lake Vue.

"Where are we going?" I asked.

"I figured we'd split a pizza, if that's all right. My stove's got problems."

"Sure."

"How's everything at your place?"

"Fine," I said.

"I know your mother doesn't like it there."

"It's okay."

"She says you're a big help," he said, but I didn't bite.

We passed the county fairgrounds and its sign advertising the same three days in August and stopped at a plaza where there was a Fox's Pizza Den. My father ordered for us. I thought he'd meant takeout, but he peeled off his coat and arranged it over a chair, and I did likewise. I wondered if he was living with this woman and didn't want me to see or whether he thought—correctly—that I would compare his apartment to ours and count it as further proof that he was cheating us.

It was not a remarkable meal. We were both hungry and embarrassed, and once the pizza came, said little. My father did not offer me a beer.

"Your mother says you have a girlfriend."

"No," I said.

"Working on it."

"Sort of."

"Want more?"

"No thanks," I said.

On the way back, my father said he had to stop by

his place for something. This made sense to me. His mistress—at the time the only word I knew to describe her—would have cleaned up and cleared out.

But when we got to Lake Vue, my father parked the car and said he'd be right back. Colored floodlights bathed the front of the complex aqua. My father's apartment was on the first floor beside a tunnel with an ice machine. He stopped at his door and hunched over his keys. In the quiet of the car I wondered what he was hiding from me, and like a sign, the bag of his crap in the backseat shifted.

I got out and flipped the seat forward and tossed the bag over my shoulder, nudged the door closed with my toe. There was a white Eldorado a few spots down, but the other cars were Fairlanes and Biscaynes and Satellites from the same era as my aunt's Nova. On the walk a broken beer bottle glittered.

The door to my father's apartment was open a sliver, just enough to see light, a nap of lemon-lime shag carpet. I swung the bag in front of me as if it were a shield or weapon and stepped in, almost knocking over an unplugged space heater.

"Hello?" my father called—beside me, behind the closed bathroom door. "Arthur?"

"Dad?" I said, but I was not answering him, I was questioning him and exactly what I was looking at.

The first thing I noticed was the rec room couch

against the wall in what I thought was the living room. It had sheets draped over its cushions, a pillow at one end, at the head a stack of library books. On the floor lay one of my old sleeping bags. In a corner stood the wicker peacock throne, beside it Astrid's old dresser. His locked toolbox. That was all, there was nothing else but rug. I took a step into the room to see what the kitchen was like, but there wasn't one, just as there was no bedroom; the paneling went all the way around, no windows or doors, not even a closet. In the near corner a hotplate sat on an end table, a cardboard box of saucepans beneath it, another box of cans. A dusting of orange powder said he'd had macaroni and cheese recently. Paper plates, one set of silverware in a motel glass, a lidded mug from Dunkin' Donuts. It was clean and, except for the sleeping bag on the floor, neat. There was really nothing wrong with it.

"Arty," my father said from the bathroom.

"I brought your things in," I said, retreating, and kicked the space heater.

He came out of the bathroom, buckling up. "This is what I didn't want you to see."

"It looks okay," I protested.

"That's nice of you." He surveyed the room as if I might be right. "Let's not tell your mother about this. She has enough worries."

"Sure," I said.

He picked up the space heater and herded me toward the door.

In the car he said, "I don't plan on being there long," and in his completely unconvincing tone I recognized my own hopes.

"So," he said next to the coachlight, "we'll keep this between us."

I was leaning down to his window and holding the space heater.

"And tell Ast I miss her."

"I will," I said, and he patted my hand.

My mother was watching from the window. When I was halfway up the stairs, she came outside to see what I was carrying.

"Why, that's just what we need," she exclaimed, and waved after my father's car, its taillights swallowed by the dark pines.

Inside I put the heater down on the floor and hung up my coat.

"Did you have a good time?" my mother asked.

"Yeah," I said, and headed for my room, though I knew she'd follow me.

S I X

ANNIE FINDS THE MITTEN at the foot of the drive. Tara has a runny nose and shouldn't be out too long, but all afternoon she'd been bugging Annie about the snow, standing at the front window watching it fall. Brock's back on days and the club's closed, getting ready for the Turkey Trot. They've been stuck in the house all week; the Maverick won't go. Brock thinks the fuel line is frozen, or maybe it's the battery. It pisses Annie off; Glenn would know. "I want my snowsuit on. I want to make a fort." She couldn't put Tara off forever.

Annie is sick herself, the flu has her couchbound, a flat glass of ginger ale by her head; otherwise she'd have been outside with Tara. Annie said ten minutes, then, groggy from the Nytol, drifted off watching "All My Children." When she woke up "General Hospital" was on.

"Ta-ra!" she calls.

The dead stalks rustle. Fields swell into distance, cut by iced-over creeks leaning with weed trees. Power lines dip away, spidery towers stride off into fog. The snow shrouds the horizon in white. It's been like this all day.

Annie steps onto the road and calls both ways, arms crossed, holding her bathrobe to her chest. She has long johns on and Brock's boots, unlaced. Trails of snow fine as sand snake over the road. The mail's here, in the box a Thrift Drug circular with holly on the front. Monday the county plowed and spread the road with grit; now it's white save a brown hump down the center. Annie can barely make out the skinny tracks of the mail Jeep among several others closing over, a flame-shaped hole left by the exhaust where Mr. Werner stopped to reach for the box. Immediately she thinks of Glenn and the restraining order they threatened to get. She hasn't let him see Tara since the fight. He's been calling and apologizing, demanding his rights. He's not dangerous, Brock says, just pathetic. Now Annie isn't sure.

She runs around the side of the house clumsily, the boots flopping. "Tara!" she calls. "Tare?" Beneath the water tower the road ends at a striped guardrail. Three or four times during the summer Annie saw a man in a blue car parked in the turnaround. A plain car, official-looking. The first time she spied him reading the *Eagle* she assumed he was from the water department, then noticed how old he was. Clare Hardesty asked her cousin the cop; no one seemed to know him. Annie figured he was harmless, a retiree trying to get out of the house. Now she sees him watching her and Tara splashing in the baby pool, his hand behind the raised newspaper, working.

"Tara," Annie shouts into the trees, "this is no time for games."

She listens to her own voice die, waits in the silence for a giggle, a twig, the rubbing of her snowsuit. Far off, a truck gears up on the interstate, and she starts for the backyard.

Rounding the corner, she stumbles and falls hard,

biting her tongue. She feels it yet forgets the pain immediately. The back is white. The snowman the two of them made yesterday leans forward, nods as if looking for its lost carrot nose, fallen and already covered. Soft ghosts of footprints scamper under the clothes carousel. It's impossible to tell today's from yesterday's, they're nearly filled in. Bomber's old house is odorless in the cold, his chain hanging from a rusty nail in the sycamore. She stands looking at the edge of the woods, arms limp, breathing steam. The trees are bare, a few birds gliding above the tangle, lighting and calling. The paths in back run clear around Marsden's Pond and up to the interstate. She can hear the trucks better here, the whine of their chains.

The porch is empty, jammed with summer junk. Annie runs around the last side of the house, fingers numb now. She's not in the car. Annie slams the door as if the Maverick's guilty, and it's cold enough that the window explodes, filling the driver's seat with snow and blue cubes. "No," Annie cries, "you shit," but doesn't have time to mourn. She looks up and down the road again, in the ditches, then sprints inside.

It is dark to save on the electric. Plastic sheets cover the windows; the winter glow makes the carpet look ratty. She turns down "General Hospital" and calls through the downstairs. The lunch dishes wait by the sink, Tara's plate with its bear hanging on to a rising bunch of balloons, an elbow straw nodding out of the matching cup. She goes through the rooms, runs upstairs. "Honey, don't hide from Mommy," she calls. The bunny Glenn bought sits in Tara's rocking chair, a carrot stitched to its paw. The shower curtain draws back on rubber flowers. She gets a rug burn looking under their bed, finds Barbie's blouse and, with it in one hand and the mitten in the other, heads for the front door, repeating her name.

Outside, the snow won't let up. Annie follows the path back toward Marsden's Pond for a few hundred feet, but when she reaches the top of the knoll over-looking it, sees nothing. The snow has chased off the kids from the high school. She needs her own boots and gloves to go any farther. She needs to call Brock. She turns and runs back toward the house.

"Overlook Home," a receptionist answers. She tells Annie to calm down, asks the name again.

"It's an emergency," Annie says.

"I'm sorry," the woman says, "he's already left for the day."

"How long ago?"

"I don't know."

Annie sees the mitten sitting next to the phone, a

few beads of melted snow clinging to the wool, and can't think of the question she needs to ask next. "It's an emergency," she tries again.

"Do you need an ambulance?" the woman asks. "Do you need the police?"

Without answering her, Annie hangs up and calls her mother.

"I'm coming," her mother says. "I'll be there in twenty minutes depending on the roads. Call what's-her-name—your neighbor."

"Clare."

"Call Clare," her mother says.

"Should I call the police?" Annie asks.

Her mother hesitates, then says, "Yes, I think that would be wise."

At lunch Brock gets stoned in his car with Tricia from payroll. The windshield is covered with snow; no one can see them. Tricia is heavy and blond and fun and from Ford City. She loves Neil Young.

"I'm living with Kenny," she says, "but when it's permanent I'll feel it, you know?"

"And it's not right now," Brock says. They have fifteen minutes left, and he's wondering if he has enough vacation time to take a half day.

"Kenny? Are you kidding? We went to school together."

"Same with me and Annie." The heater cranks, a leaf stuck in the fan. Smoke leaks out the window. She likes him, he knows; she lets him look into her eyes. It's more than attraction on his part. He's never been with a woman this big, has never considered it before. The possibility itself seems a bounty. He has been trying to figure out why he thinks he is in love with her. He wants to accept it, give in, make a fool of himself. He's got to get out of Annie's, it's too crazy; she always wants to talk about Barb, about how he didn't have to hurt Glenn. Brock doesn't want to abandon Annie but Tricia may be expecting something more than friendship. He's ready for a change, a break. Hell, he's lying to himself, he's dreaming.

"The Needle and the Damage Done" takes him inside the dash, into some lost summer night, a dark back road. The roach falls apart. Tricia has gum and gives him a stick. He checks the sideview mirror. Behind them a few cars cruise for a spot; the front office people are getting back from the Hot Dog Shoppe, Natili's, Hojo's. He reaches over to put his Visine back in the glove compartment, and Tricia meets and then kisses him, the gum sweet between their tongues.

"What are we going to do about this?" she says.

Clare has the car because it's Friday, and Friday her mother, Regina, visits her friends at the Overlook Home. Regina used to live there, but a few months ago she asked if she could come home, and when Jerrell and Clare said no, refused to eat. Now she sees her friends three times a week and they have to pay twice as much for her dinner. They're on their way out the door when Annie calls, and Clare has no choice but to bring Regina. They can check the fields and woods down by the pond and then, if they haven't found her, drive around looking.

Annie says she doesn't have a better plan.

"Lost?" Regina says when Clare gets off the phone. "How do you lose your only child?"

"I'm sure it's a mix-up," Clare says. "Her father probably has her right now."

"That's not the child's father she's living with?" Clare knows she knows; Regina's only saying it to point out how wrong it is.

"That's her young man."

Regina shakes her head. "He cleans bedpans for a living."

"We're leaving, Mother."

Outside, after Clare scrapes the Bonneville off, it stalls on her. It's given her trouble before; she keeps telling Jerrell it's going to die soon.

"You might try the choke," Regina says.

"Do you see a choke?" Clare asks, but it's pointless, Regina can barely see to read. Annie's is only across the road and down a half mile; they could almost coast. Turkey Hill used to go to Saxonburg until they put the highway in. Sometimes Clare thinks she would like the privacy. She cranks the starter and the engine turns over, protesting; she gives it a little extra, revs it, and starts down the drive.

She turns onto Turkey Hill and the water tank looms, giant, blue.

Clare sees Annie waving by the mailbox, hatless, hair a tangle, flat on one side. Jerrell is always asking Clare why she bothers; the girl is trouble, anyone can see that.

"Oh," Clare says, "and how do you see trouble?"

"Easy," Jerrell says, "you just look. There it is— trouble."

"You don't even know her," Clare says. "She's very nice." But Annie is not very nice, is not a friend like the one Clare imagined when Mrs. Peterson's family decided to cart her off to Florida. She is young in all the wrong ways; she never knows when to stop.

She treated Glenn like trash, for Brock, and from what Clare has seen (and sometimes she likes what she sees: Brock doesn't worry about the oil bill, he likes the night life, the strip beside the Pullman works), Brock isn't the marrying kind. Like Jerrell, she asks herself what Annie could possibly be getting out of it. Her answer changes when Jerrell collapses on her, sour-breathed from his three beers watching the Penguin game, musky from climbing all day. He is a lineman for the phone company, and at times Clare dreams of dialing a fatal number, a bolt of energy that will reach him wherever he is around the county and knock him, safety belt and all, senseless through the wires. She loves him, she supposes, or else why would she still be here—not for Warren's sake, he's never listened to her. Where else would she go? But thinking like this is silly; she is not going anywhere. She does love the idiot. She is not perfect. She would have settled for Glenn.

Clare slows for Annie. "Mother," she says, "you're going to have to sit on the hump."

"Is this her?" Regina says.

Annie climbs in, her face chafed from crying, and for the first time since she called, Clare realizes this is not a mistake, a simple mix-up.

"We'll look at the pond first," Clare says. She waits for Annie's okay, then drives to the turnaround and bumps over the crushed curb and onto the dirt road. She follows it down along the treeline, shuddering over the frozen, rutted mud.

Regina holds on to the dashboard. "I don't think the car was built for this."

"Don't talk," Clare says, "look."

The fields are bare, last year's late corn cropped in rows, a few bent and bleached survivors waving limply. The radio is on to get the weather; the real snow is still holding off, it's too cold yet. At the corner of the field a dirt mound sprouting old fenceposts blocks the road.

Clare puts it in park.

"I'll stay here," her mother says. Annie is already out and headed down toward the pond.

"Give a honk every few minutes," Clare instructs. "That way we can't get lost."

"Roger Wilco."

Clare runs to catch up.

May grabs a Tupperware carton of barley soup from the deep freeze in the basement, two twenties she keeps in her next-best teapot, and her purse, and is out the door and on the road. The Polara wobbles over the snow; there's something wrong with the steering but she doesn't have time to worry about it. She pictures Tara in her powder blue jacket with the fur-trimmed hood, wandering among the trees—when that is the best thing that can happen. She tries not to think of a van slowing and stopping, a pair of hands. Or Tara on the ground, twigs caught in her white tights.

The Polara is so slow that it must be the engine. She gets caught behind a truck, and then at a railroad crossing, endless black hoppers of coal.

"Goddammit!" she yells at the flashing red lights. "Let's go!"

In her heart she knows it's not Glenn. She is more worried about Brock taking advantage of Annie. It's all of a piece, she thinks. Her daughter's life is in such disorder; it's killing her. A three-year-old and no way to support herself. How she is getting the rent May doesn't know, certainly not from what she makes at the club. Every time she asks Annie they end up fighting. She has always felt—though never said, or only to Charles, softened—that Annie is not a very smart person, that she doesn't look ahead and then is surprised when things go wrong. Raymond did a stint in the Marines, and Dennis paid his way through the community college. Annie still seems to be back in high school, working part-time, picking which boy she will give herself to. She is their youngest, and according to everything May has read, she should be clinging to Annie for dear life. May just wishes she would settle down, or if that will never happen (and she fears this, her only girl), move away where she won't have to see it. But how she would miss Tara.

The man in the car beside her at the crossing has rolled down his window and is shouting at her.

May fumbles with the crank. The train clanks and thunders, and she can't hear him. "What?"

"You got a flat tire," he points.

"Thank you," May nods, then when the gate rises, guns across the tracks.

She swings into the first service station she sees—a Phillips 66—and honks for the attendant to take care of her. As she's waiting, a state trooper shoots by, siren wailing. She pictures Annie slamming Tara against the oven and can't stop her next thought: I hope she hasn't done anything.

It's a busy day at work for Glenn. The last nationwide catalogue of the year went out two weeks ago, and now the orders are pouring in. Most are common, things they have clean pieces for—'57 Chevys and

Shelby Cobras, Goats, Tempests—but four or five times a day some customer wonders if they might have an item he didn't see listed. Since Glenn is new, he's the one that has to buckle the tool belt on over his coat and drive the golf cart through the snow until he finds the car and the part they want.

The wrecks are arranged by make—Fords here, Mercurys next to them, big Lincolns—then broken down in lines by model. Sometimes Glenn dawdles to make the day go faster, lingers over the dead motor or in the bloodied seats, but today it's freezing and he's trying to make up for being late. Last night he and Rafe stayed up until three. He remembers Rafe trying to convince him to stop going to church and that they smashed some glasses, but only part of the ride home. When he woke up, he saw that Bomber had gotten sick on the jeans he'd been saving. Hot dogs. In the mirror his lip was still purple, the cut under his eye crusted.

"Who are you calling a quitter?" he said, but when he opened the medicine cabinet there were no aspirin.

Now he's searching for a taillight and bracket for a '62 Oldsmobile F-85, an ugly little turtle of a car long since discontinued. He drives straight to the GM section along the far fence and makes a right past the Buicks and Cadillacs and Chevys. The faster he goes, the colder his face gets, even through the itchy ski mask. Beneath him the cart whirs. He reaches the Cutlasses and slows. Delta 88's. The wrecks watch him, some one-eyed, blind, snow caked on their bumpers and hoods and roofs. The F-85's start, a whole row of them. He knows there's a green '62 out here somewhere.

"Yes," he says, spying it. He takes his foot off the gas and the motor of the golf cart automatically stops. Glenn likes it out here; it's quiet, only the snow sifting into the trees and tangle beyond the fence.

He goes to the rear of the car and brushes snow from the trunk. Both lights are intact. The customer only wanted one, but which one? The right and left assemblies are slightly different. Glenn decides to save himself a trip and remove both.

He's working on a frozen bolt with some WD40 and a hexhead screwdriver when he hears something crunch behind the Ramblers. He straightens up and looks around. It can be spooky out here too, all the splintered windshields and sheared steering columns.

"Nothing," he says. Wind. He bends to the task again.

"Glenn Marchand," a stern voice calls, and he thinks, in the time it takes him to locate it, that it might be from the sky.

"Drop the screwdriver," a trooper behind an Ambassador calls. He has a gun but pointed straight up. "Take off the belt and come out from there now."

Glenn does, and another man in an expensive trenchcoat spins him around to face the hood and knees him against the fender. He flashes his ID, says his name is Inspector Burns. "Hands on the car," he says. He yanks Glenn's ski mask off, stubbing his nose. "Now get flat for me. Get flat."

Glenn doesn't understand, and the inspector takes him by the scruff of the neck and gently bends him over the hood. Glenn lays his cheek against the snow. His lip throbs. The inspector lifts his wallet and keys, pats him down and tells him to get up. A trooper in a marked unit pulls alongside.

"What did I do?" Glenn says.

"Nothing, we hope," the inspector says. "Your daughter is missing."

"What?" Glenn says, but a trooper has his arm and is leading him toward the open door, the fenced-off backseat. "What's going on?"

"Is this your most recent picture?" the inspector asks from the front. He's holding the shot of Tara Glenn carries in his wallet.

"It's brand-new," Glenn says. "I've got tons of them at home."

Regina looks at the clock on the dash. Clare and Annie have only been gone a few minutes, but she expects them to appear at the end of the trail any second, carrying a tearful Tara. It is amazing to Regina that something like this hasn't happened already, the way the girl lives. Cast the first stone, but in this case the woman is an outright tramp, sleeping around on her husband and then taking up with a no-good. And from a perfectly nice family, that's the terrible thing. What her mother must go through every time she thinks of her. She knows May Van Dorn for a good woman. How her daughter turned out this way is a mystery, an honest-to-goodness shame. Regina hopes it is a black sheep thing, a wild gene, that Annie will turn out a Van Dorn. And who knows, this thing could teach Annie a lesson, turn her around. It is not the just but the sinner God rejoices in saving. The forecast calls for 3 to 6 inches, 6 to 8 in the mountains. Regina checks the clock, reaches over and honks the horn.

On the path above the pond, Annie hears it, distant through the trees. The path is icy, and several times Annie falls hard. She stops and looks back over the pond, the water tower rising above the woods, the fields to the north. Flakes drift down, drawn sharp by the dark, solid sky. Far off, white ranches shine, barns lean. The tamed fairways of the country club surround the low stone clubhouse, the emptied pool a blue dot. She has never been this far back, though she has known of the shortcut since middle school. The view makes everything seem even stranger. She spots Clare's green-and-black mackinaw in the brush below the spillway, tiny. There is no way Tara could make it up this hill, she thinks, but she keeps climbing, falling and getting up again as the whoosh and rush of the highway nears.

She scissors over the guardrail. The ground is dry up here, and walking's easy. A shred of truck tire lies on the gravel berm. The two sets of lanes are salt-stained, the snow in the dip of the median gray but virgin. She jogs against traffic toward an overpass a half mile away—the footbridge between the two schools. A semi passes in the right lane, and the wind following knocks her back a step; gravel peppers her shins. A bleached beer case wheels in the air above her and lands. She passes a few wrenched and flattened pipes, rusting. Over the guardrail the embankment is sheer now, the treetops at eye level. Holding on to the sooty steel lip, Annie peers down. Twenty feet below her, stuck in a crotch, sags a dead deer.

She puts a hand to her throat to stop the vomit, but

it comes. She goes to her hands and knees and chokes it out, careful of her hair. She doesn't have time for this, she thinks, and gets up before she's done, makes it a few steps and doubles over. Before she tries again she wipes her eyes; she doesn't want to wander onto the road.

By the time she reaches the footbridge she's fine. The fence around the bottom is bent at the top from kids climbing over; it's easily too high for Tara. Annie hears the horn—sounding not once but continuously —and runs back down the berm toward it. They've found her, she thinks, then hopes against hope, not wanting to jinx it.

She vaults the guardrail and starts down the path, taking baby steps, searching for the green dot of Clare below. The horn blares in the woods. On the steep part Annie slips. She's going too fast, and as she's falling tries to slide. She sticks her arms out to grab hold of something or at least slow herself down, but there's nothing but snow. Below, the path turns and there is a sheer drop into trees. She's on her side now, bouncing, picking up speed. Her jacket has hiked up; snow scrapes and burns at her waist. She sees the bend coming and tries to plant her feet, to dig her fingers in, but her elbow catches a rock, and reflexively she curls around the hurt. The path turns, and she shoots off the curve, suddenly airborne.

Miraculously, she misses the trees, lands farther down the slope, rolling over and over in the snow. She's surprised she's all right. The horn is still going. Annie stands and shrugs off the snow, plants a foot, then feels the ankle give. She can walk on it.

"Are you okay?" Clare calls from the bottom of the hill.

"Fine," Annie waves. No, it's broken. "Why is your mother honking?"

"The police are here."

"Do they get cable?" Tricia asks, naked, sipping wine from the tiny sanitized glass. They have been making love all afternoon, using both beds, filling the room with sweet smoke. They have the heat blasting and the lights out; the white outside sneaks in around the blinds, and when someone walks by, shadows ripple across the back wall.

"There's never anything on in the day," Brock says. He tongues her navel, trying to get her to spill. She throws the cupful over him and he yelps, then, laughing, dives across her and grabs the bottle off the nightstand.

"Don't waste it."

"We've got another."

"We don't want to make a mess," she says. "Someone has to clean these rooms."

"How about the tub?" Brock says.

"That could be fun." Tricia hops off the bed. He watches her walk into the bathroom, hears the knobs squeak and the water running.

Looking at the whirled stucco of the ceiling, Brock thinks of Tara crying herself to sleep last night because Annie didn't give her a bath.

It all started when they were watching "Let's Make a Deal." Tara was in the kitchen and asked if she could have an M&M. "A red one?" she said.

"No," Annie said, "because you didn't finish your dinner."

"Oh, give her one," he said. He thought she was being bitchy because she was sick.

"No. She didn't eat her dinner, why should she have candy?" Annie leaned her head back, listening. "You better not be eating M&M's out there."

"Would she?" Brock asked.

"In a minute. Tara?" she called. "Tara?" They both went into the kitchen and found Tara under the table, her cheeks crammed, a brown string of drool on her chin. "Come out here now," Annie said. "Now! You come when I say." She yanked her out by the arm, and Tara's head hit the bottom of the table. The child began to cry, red-faced and gulping, showing the brown cud. Annie began to spank her hard on the bottom.

"Hold on," Brock said, "hold on."

"You stay the fuck out of this," she said, pointing. Tara's face was ugly with tears. Her lip quivered as she tried to get her breath back. "Go watch your goddamn show," Annie said, and he did.

And then ten minutes later it was all forgotten, forgiven. Brock can't understand how the two of them do it. Over nothing. Later when they were going up to bed, Annie said, "No bath," and Tara threw herself to the floor and pitched a fit. "You see?" Annie said, and spanked her again, calmly this time. Downstairs they heard her wailing well into the nine o'clock movie.

He did the right thing staying out of it—she's her mother—but now Brock wishes he had stopped her. Rarely does he have to yell at Tara when they're together; she's a good kid. Annie says he's easy because he's not responsible for her, implying that he never will be, that he is going to leave. While it's true, Brock thinks it's no excuse. Next time he'll step between them and, if necessary, take the punishment himself.

In the bathroom the knobs squeak and the water stops.

"Everything's ready," Tricia calls. "I'm just waiting for you."

Brock pushes himself out of bed and turns the TV off, and there he is in the mirror again. The other Brock in the other room looks to him as if waiting for an answer. As if there is one.

Annie wakes up in bed with her clothes on, her boots off, the one ankle wrapped with an Ace bandage. Gray light fights through the plastic; the room seems tired, the clothes in a heap, the scattered toys. Talk seeps up from downstairs. She remembers the man at the ambulance saying her ankle was badly sprained. He was giving her something for the pain when she fainted.

"Brock?" she calls.

There is a knock, and then a policewoman looks in. "Your husband is on the way. Can I get you anything?"

"What husband?" Annie says.

"You're not married?"

"We're separated. He didn't have Tara?"

"Your daughter, no."

"Then why aren't you looking for her?"

"We have people out and we'll have the Lifeflight helicopter from the hospital if the weather holds off.

We're trying to do everything. Do you want to go out? I'm supposed to accompany you if you do. My name is Officer Scott.''

"Where's Brock?'' Annie asks.

"Who?''

Glenn waits with Inspector Burns in the kitchen while the men go through the house. His father and mother sit at the table; they've given their permission, offered the inspector coffee. The floor is wet with bootprints. Out back Bomber is loud. The inspector has promised they will take Glenn to Annie's to join the search after they're done here. Glenn has told him it's a waste of time; they could be out looking. Though he has no handcuffs on, he feels paralyzed, out of control. He needs to pee.

A uniformed trooper pulls up in Glenn's truck. He walks around the arc of Bomber's chain, carrying a manila envelope. The inspector opens the door for him, takes the envelope. It's stuffed thick as a pillow with plastic bags.

"They're mostly dog hair.''

"Get pictures?'' the inspector asks.

Glenn worries that he hasn't washed the seats well enough, that they'll pick up blood in the upholstery.

He's told the inspector about the fight ("Where'd you get the lip?" he asked), but feels it's only put him under deeper suspicion.

And he has been back to the old house, if only to watch the lights from the edge of the field. It's his family; he can't stay away. They'll match his tire tracks, ask his parents where he goes at night.

The troopers' boots rumble upstairs. His bladder stings. Holding it is distracting him, giving him a head-ache.

"I don't know why you think he has anything to do with this," his mother says.

"Livvie."

"No. This is my house. You should be asking her. She won't even let him see his own daughter."

"It's true," his father admits, as if it's a secret. "He hasn't been able to see her two straight weeks now."

"That's what your son told me," the inspector says.

"Doesn't that tell you something?" his mother says.

A trooper in a bulky flak jacket comes in from the living room with a pair of double-barreled shotguns broken over his shoulders, and Glenn's father gets up.

"Those were my father's," he says, "and I don't appreciate you or anybody touching them."

"Ithacas," the inspector notes, intervening. "They *are* old. Knickerbockers. Beautiful guns." He sniffs both breeches and, careful of their barrels, hands them gently to Glenn's father. "Very sorry," he says. "All of this is routine. I promise we will get you to the site as soon as we can."

"Can I use the bathroom?" Glenn asks.

"Where is it?" the inspector says.

He follows Glenn in and, while Glenn goes, stands facing the other way, watching his eyes.

"You're capable," the inspector says. "You could do it."

"Do what?"

"Take her from her mother. Tell me you wouldn't."

"I would never hurt Tara." Glenn doesn't like the way he says this—stagey, fake. It's ridiculous to even talk about it.

"That's not what I'm saying," the inspector says.

"I didn't do anything."

"I know that. But you've thought of it."

"No," Glenn says, "I haven't," and wonders if he's telling the truth.

In the kitchen his mother is wrapping the hamburg she's been thawing for dinner. She has her coat on. His father's gone out to warm the car. When the troopers come downstairs, the house shakes.

"So?" his mother taunts.

"We've seen everything we need to see for now."

Glenn rides with the inspector in an unmarked car, his parents following a cruiser in the Fury. The defrost is on; flakes hit the windshield and disappear. On the dash sits a blue bubble like the one in his truck. He thinks of a girl Tara's age he saved when he was working rescue. She'd been swimming in a plastic blow-up pool when her mother had to go answer the phone. Glenn spread her out on the lawn and administered CPR. He remembers feeling contempt for the woman, just as now he feels contempt for himself at not being able to protect Tara. It is, to some extent, his fault.

"Marchand," the inspector says, "you want to tell me about the picture?"

"What picture?"

"Your drawing, the one over your bed."

He means a sketch Elder Francis asked him to make during his counseling. How do you envision your personal relationship with Jesus? In it, the world is represented by a city under a sea of blood, the people chained to each other. Glenn shows himself drowning; the bubbles coming out of his mouth join into a blue ghost that floats up to heaven and whispers into the smiling Christ's ear.

"It means I'm saved," Glenn says.

"From what?"

"The world. Hell. Everything."

"That's a lot to ask from one guy," the inspector says.

"It's not like I have a choice," Glenn says.

Turning into Turkey Hill with the entourage, he sees a line of men slowly combing the fields. The house is surrounded by cars—police, an ambulance, the rescue truck. Closer, he notices Brock's Charger's not there and that the Maverick's window is broken. Immediately he thinks they've had a fight (over him, perhaps, over Tara). The inspector tells Glenn to wait until he comes around and opens the door.

"I don't want you and the missis starting anything," he warns. "Do and you're gone."

But inside, with so many people around, Annie is quiet. She sits on the couch with her wrapped foot up on the coffee table, on one side her mother, on the other a policewoman he recognizes from a recent trailer fire. The door's open and it's cold. The squawk and static of walkie-talkies is constant. Inspector Burns stands just in front of him, as if ready to step in.

"You don't have her," Annie asks, but it's not an accusation. She looks exhausted.

"What happened?" he says.

"She just wandered off," May explains.

"Swear to me, Glenn. You don't have her."

"I wouldn't do something like that."

"We picked him up at his work," Inspector Burns confirms.

"Where's Brock?" Glenn asks.

May throws her hands up in disgust.

"I don't know. He was supposed to be at the Home but they say he isn't there."

"We have people en route," the policewoman says.

The bastard, Glenn thinks, guessing right.

"Go look for her," Annie says, "you know where she'd go."

"Can I?" Glenn asks the inspector, who then calls a trooper over to shadow him.

"Find her," Annie says.

"I will," Glenn promises.

Barb is finishing her shift at the Rusty Nail when Roy Barnum walks in, takes a stool and orders a decaf, milk and sugar. He's on duty and it's free, house rule. Barb draws it off the urn, clanks it down. Roy slides a flyer across the counter, a grainy photograph in the center, a little girl in overalls, puffy cheeks, devilish smile.

"Put this up in a good spot for me?" Roy asks, but Barb has recognized Tara and, with one hand covering her mouth, stands speechless.

The road is lined with police cars—some state, Brock sees—and quickly weighing turning around, he double-parks in front of the house and hurries over the snow. Glenn. He imagines what he will have to do if Annie is dead. He thinks he will be heartbroken but in time recover. This is insane.

The yard is full of cops, one of them talking to Glenn.

"Brock," Glenn says as if he's his friend.

"What's going on?" Brock asks the cop.

"Are you the boyfriend?"

"Where's Annie?"

"Tara is missing," Glenn says, as if it's his fault.

Annie is inside, sitting with her mother. He wants to go to her but her mother won't let him through. He wonders if they can smell the soap on him, the wine through his Juicy Fruit. Tara is missing. Nothing in the world goes right for him.

"Where the fuck were you?" Annie says.

"Work."

"No you weren't."

A cop in a trenchcoat comes over and asks if he is Brock.

"Yes," Brock says, sick of this shit, "I am Brock."

The snow comes down sideways, blowing, smoothing over footprints in minutes. The Lifeflight is grounded. There is only another hour of light, and already it is poor. The woods crackle with volunteers. The news is on the radio; Rafe comes straight from work. The Friday AA meeting is here, the Women's Methodist Alliance. Clare and Jerrell search the cannibalized pickups and tractors at the north edge of the cornfield; Brock and Glenn are with the inspector down below the pond. May and Regina, Frank and Olive talk in the living room, the public-access channel with its thermometer and clock on silently beside them. Barb has taped Tara's flyer to the mirror of the Rusty Nail and driven out in her uniform, bare legs, heels and all. The hunt has spread across the interstate to the middle school grounds. Trucks file by the flares, the troopers' orange-coned flashlights. The Army Reserve has promised two squads if this should go until tomorrow.

Yet it will not be any of these searchers who finds Tara, but a fourteen-year-old from the high school marching band, small for his size, generally ignored, in fact, myself, Arthur Parkinson, who, because she is dead, will not be a hero—will not, years from now, even be remembered around town as the one who found her—but who, with Annie and Glenn and Brock and May and Frank and Olive and Clare and Barb, will find Tara again and again throughout his life and never ever lose her.

S E V E N

I REMEMBER NOT WANTING TO GO. It was a Friday and we had just taken the field. Thanksgiving we were playing Armstrong Township; in the cafeteria banners urged us to JUMP THE BEAVERS. We were standing around in groups warming up with rock riffs—"Satisfaction," "Foxy Lady"—when the vice-principal came running over the footbridge. Mr. Chervenick blew his whistle and climbed the roll-away podium. We would make this up next Monday, he said, regardless of the weather. He stressed that participation in the search was not mandatory.

"Yeah right," Warren said beside me.

No one in the band was cool or vicious enough to call Mr. Chervenick's bluff. Most of us in the brass were glad; on a day so cold, it took faith to put your lips to the mouthpiece. We snapped our cases shut and marched back over the bridge. Two buses waited for us, chugging out clouds in the snow. We were to leave our instruments and bookbags in the lobby; the janitor would watch them.

The vice-principal, Mr. Eisenstat, rode with us. He brought the lost-and-found box and walked the aisle, asking if anyone needed gloves. We would need them, he said, when we got to the site.

"The site," Warren gravely mimicked. We sat together in back under the curved sea-green ceiling, burnt from a long day's partying. It was a Friday, which meant a celebration, and next week was Thanksgiving.

Neither fact made me happy. Band days I didn't get to walk home from the bus stop with Lila, and weekends, though we lived in adjacent buildings, I didn't see her. Schoolnights I lay awake thinking of what I would say to her the next morning, of how I would ask her to a movie. That never happened, of course, but Friday nights that winter seemed to me especially hopeless.

As for Thanksgiving, my mother hinted that this year we might not have dinner with my father's parents in Pittsburgh. Slyly she'd been feeling me out about the Horn of Plenty, a buffet down Route 8 we used to go to for her birthday. It was all-you-can-eat. At the end of the steamtable a cook in a chef's toque sliced a bloody roast beef under a heat lamp. I said it would be okay, but in a grunt, meaning it wasn't.

"Look," my mother snapped, "maybe you haven't noticed, but things are different now."

"I've noticed," I said.

"Then just save your little smart-ass comments. I'm trying to tell you this as nicely as I can. Your father doesn't seem to be showing much interest in doing anything as a family this year. I'd like to because I think it would be nice for you, but when I call your father and try to talk about it, all he does is put me off. I am going to try to set things up the way they've been, but I'm warning you that it might not happen. Now would you like that or should I just not bother?"

"Whatever," I said.

"Whatever," my mother challenged.

"It's okay, I don't care."

"I don't know why I try," she said. "Obviously it means nothing to you that I have to ask these people to do us a favor when I would rather not talk to them at all."

"It does mean something," I said, but too late; she had turned away and plopped down on the couch and was lighting a cigarette. "The Horn of Plenty's fine."

"That's shit," my mother said, tossing her lighter at the table. It slid across a magazine and dropped to the carpet. My mother turned on the TV and wouldn't look at me.

I'd seen and, more often, heard her fight like this with my father, but I had never been on the receiving end, and felt—rightfully or not—that she was taking advantage of my inexperience. I didn't know how to fight back. The next morning she acted as if nothing had happened. I was still angry. Like the child I was, I was keeping score.

Warren, my only confidant, said mothers get nutty around holidays. We discussed it on the bus on the way over to the site. He was tired of my negativity, he said. We had blown a serious bone in the parking lot after last period, hoping to make practice bearable, and we were pronouncing on the world at large.

"Let's say you're your mother."

"Let's say," I said.

"Okay, now I'm you and Thanksgiving is coming up. 'I hate Thanksgiving, I don't care if we have turkey, I don't give a shit.' I mean, is that what she wants to hear?"

"You mean me."

"Yeah," he said.

"I don't say it like that. And that's not the point. She thinks she's doing me this big favor when she's not."

"Oh, so you want to go to the Horn of Plenty and eat cheese cubes for Thanksgiving."

"My mother does."

"You."

"Me if I'm my mother."

"Where do you want to eat for Thanksgiving?" Warren asked.

"I don't care," I said.

"Fuck you."

"Yeah," I said, "that's pretty much what she said."

"She's right. I don't see why you're all pissed off."

We crossed the interstate. Mr. Eisenstat came down the aisle, passing out flyers with a picture of the little girl. I didn't like her first name and didn't recognize the last. Mr. Eisenstat held up the flyer and spoke so we could all hear, even those of us like Warren and myself who were not interested. Everything he told us was on the flyer except one.

"She has been missing for between two and three hours."

Warren looked out at the snow, looked back at me and shook his head. "She's meat."

"Frozen food," I said. "Now look who's being negative."

We didn't know where we were going. We hadn't gotten far when the bus slowed and swung onto a road, trees on one side, an open field on the other. A man wearing irrigators walked the iced-over ditch, stopping to test for soft spots. In the field a brace of dogs pulled a man in a hunter's cap along. People had parked off the road, facing the wrong way. Farther on was a house, but we didn't come close to getting there. The bus stopped and Mr. Millhauser said, "That's it."

"Buddy up," Mr. Eisenstat instructed. "Stay in sight of each other. We don't want you getting lost too."

"What a zeke," Warren said.

Once we were off, I saw the water tower. Mr. Chervenick marched us down the road six abreast as if we were filing through the stadium tunnel.

"We could have walked here quicker," I said.

"You still have that roach?" Warren asked.

News crews were filming, and as we passed in back of each neatly dressed reporter, we gave the entire city of Pittsburgh the finger. A Red Cross canteen truck was handing out free coffee and hot chocolate; cups blew around the parked cars' tires. We followed Mr. Chervenick past the house, unconsciously falling into step.

Orange horses blocked off the road just short of the turnaround. Police manned a long folding table with a map taped across the top, behind them a garbage can over which searchers were warming their hands. We waited at parade rest while Mr. Chervenick talked to a trooper with a clipboard. He came back and announced that we would go over an area below the pond which had already been done.

"If you find something you believe is important, do not touch it or move it. Get me or Mr. Eisenstat, and we will get the appropriate person to look at it. Please do not touch or move anything you believe is important; I can't stress that enough."

"Does everyone have a buddy?" Mr. Eisenstat asked, and when no one said anything, asked, "Who *doesn't* have a buddy?"

The woods above the pond were full of old people in black baseball caps celebrating Pullman-Standard's

70th anniversary. As we walked down the hill, the mixed group that had just searched our area passed us coming up, breathing hard.

The pond was frozen but not solid. In the middle a slick of gray water sat atop the ice. When Mr. Chervenick whistled for us to close ranks and stand at attention, we could hear the spillway.

"Everything from here down to the highway fence is our responsibility," he said. "I imagine some of you are familiar with the terrain." It got a small laugh, but not from myself or Warren. "Spread out and be thorough. This is a very small child. I will signal with five short reports for everyone to meet back here." He blew once to dismiss us.

Warren and I wandered along, careful to stick to existing prints. The snow was too cold to pack and crunched under our boots like someone grinding their teeth. I had only seen one dead person face-to-face, and that in a casket—my grandmother Sellars. My idea of a corpse came from the comic books I grew up reading—The Witching Hour, Weird War, The House of Mystery. I imagined finding the girl frozen and blue, one clutching hand sticking through the crust. Her eyes would be a transparent gray, robbed of color like a cooked onion. We inched along, looking in the snowy bushes, hoping to hear a shout from somewhere else. The bootprints stopped and so did we.

"She wouldn't be down there," Warren reasoned. "Probably in the pond."

In the woods above us a bullhorn blurted something. We both froze and waited but there was nothing. We kept going, slower now.

"So," Warren said, "do you have that roach or what?"

I looked in my box of Marlboros, stirred the cigarettes around with a finger until I spied it. It was good-sized, the paper stained dark with resin. "Where's a good place to do it?"

We both swiveled our heads for cops.

"Let's go to the pipe," Warren said, meaning where the creek went through the hillside and under the highway. The pipe was corrugated steel, around three feet wide. There was a caged storm drain beside it to draw off any extra water. The whole thing was hidden in a ditch, and when the security guards were coming you'd dive into it as if it were a foxhole and wait. You could pee there in privacy too when there was a kegger.

I hesitated, thinking it was a pretty good place for a little kid to drown.

"They probably looked there first," Warren assured me. "They've got maps."

As we made our way through the brush, we commented on the dwindling number of prints.

"At least there are some," Warren said.

"Not many," I said.

But when we reached the ditch, the snow on both sides of the creek was trampled and smudged with mud.

"See?" Warren said.

The ice on the creek stopped a few feet before the pipe. The water was high but still, brown as coffee. It poured into the storm drain with a sucking noise. Warren peeked over the rise to see if anyone was near us.

"It's cool," he said, and we sat down on the cage above the drain. I stuck the roach on an alligator clip and handed it and my mother's green Bic to Warren. He drew deeply on it and handed it back, holding the smoke in, then blew out a cloud.

"This beats the shit out of practice," he said.

I nodded, enjoying the tickle of the first hit, and handed the clip back.

"I am feeling very positive," I said. Warren nodded sagely. The rush was instant but slow, a creeping tingle along the jaw, like the surprising late heat of a spicy chili. David Larue, who'd sold me the nickel, said it was Colombian. We suspected it was Mexican. It was a little harsh but gave you a pleasant buzz, nothing too intense for a day at school.

Warren and I passed it back and forth until it went

out, then roasted it over a high flame, sucking the smoke off the blackened nub.

"You can get another hit out of it," Warren said.

"You want another?"

I knocked it off into the water. We watched the current take it hesitantly into the pipe. The motion of the roach seemed to have its own ineluctable drama and meaning. We were fucked up.

"Thanks," Warren said.

We sat in silence a moment, stoned, looking at our new surroundings.

"This is some fucked-up shit," Warren said, and I knew what he meant.

"You better look and see if any of those cops are hanging around."

"Paranoid," Warren said, but stood and looked. "Nothing."

In the water a soaked mitten floated. Pink and white, with some kind of design.

"Check out this mitten," I said.

"Don't touch it," Warren said, "you're not supposed to touch it."

Slow as a leaf, the mitten drifted over the brown water toward the pipe. I broke a branch off a bush.

"Okay," Warren said, "I guess you have to now."

The branch wasn't long enough, and I had to bend down and lean out over the water. I just touched it and

169

it floated toward the other side. With Warren behind me, I scrambled up the ditch and around and down. I couldn't quite get it from this side either. Warren went to get a bigger branch while I kept my eye on the mitten. The pipe seemed to be drawing it in the closer it got.

"Hurry up," I said. "We're going to lose it."

"I'm hurrying," Warren said.

I was kneeling at the edge of the creek, watching, when a second white mitten floated to the surface— except this mitten had fingers and was attached to a puffy blue arm. The girl's face rolled out of the water, still encased in her hood, its fur muddy, the drawstring knotted under her chin.

I ran. I ran straight up the ditch to Warren, who was fighting a bush for a green branch. I tried to tell him but nothing would come.

"There," I said. "Mud," I said. "The coat." It was like the last few seconds of "Password" when you use all the clues.

Warren took me by the arm and we walked to the top of the ditch and looked down.

She was on her back, her mouth and eyes open, drifting headfirst toward the pipe. A boot had fallen off.

We ran.

"Mister Chervenick!" Warren called.
"Mister Chervenick!" we called.

Mr. Chervenick talked with my mother while I waited in our car. As usual, she was late. It was fully night, not quite dinnertime. The snow had not stopped, and the wipers arced in rhythm, the headlights giving the falling flakes a stagey, theatrical quality. I wanted a cigarette but didn't dare in the car. Finally Mr. Chervenick opened the lobby door for my mother and she crossed in front of the hood. She got in and clicked her belt on but didn't shift into drive.

"You didn't tell me you were the one," she said.

"Me and Warren," I said.

"Are you okay?"

"Yeah."

"Mr. Chervenick said you were pretty upset."

"Right when it happened, yeah. So was Warren. So was everybody. Then they just shoved us on the bus. Some of the girls were crying."

"How about you?" my mother said.

"I was sad, I guess. I don't know."

My mother slid across the seat and held me. I endured it. Mr. Chervenick had left.

"You're okay," she asked. "You're sure."

"I'm hungry," I said.

"Do you know whose little girl that was?"

"I didn't know her name."

"That was Annie Van Dorn's little girl. You remember Annie."

I hadn't for a long time, and now that I was, the crush I had had on her returned, mixed with the image of the girl floating backwards. "Sure."

My mother told me about Annie's marriage and separation as if they were tragedies linked and equal to this one. As she was speaking, the Annie I had known seemed to vanish, to become so much older that I could not imagine what she might look like. I was still stoned and associating things freely and could not help but compare Annie's story to my mother's—the missing husband and lost child.

"I'm going to have to go see Mrs. Van Dorn," she said. "It would be nice if you came too."

I said I would.

My mother didn't tell me about her day. We passed the Van Dorns'—their lights were off—and our old house without comment. I thought of Annie coming over to babysit, jumping from her father's truck with her books, her long hair swinging.

Before getting out at Foxwood, my mother said, "You're sure you're okay?"

"I only looked at her a few seconds."

"Something like that, that's enough. I'm going to ask you to do me a favor."

"What?" I said. I was tired. I wanted to eat and watch TV.

"I want you to come with me when I see Dr. Brady next week. You'll like him, he's really very nice." She went off on a long spiel, and I knew she'd made up her mind.

"I'll go," I conceded. She held me again, sitting there in the glare from the coachlight. It seemed she could not touch me enough. When she pulled away, I could see she was crying—just a tear she wiped away with a gloved finger. She tried to smile.

"What are we having for dinner?" I asked, because I truly wanted to know and not because I thought it would make her laugh.

The next day my father unexpectedly showed up after lunch in his Nova. While it was a Saturday, we hadn't made any plans, and after our last disaster, I wasn't sure if he wanted to see me or vice versa. I was surprised that I was glad he had come. My mother asked him in for a cup of hot chocolate.

"Maybe later," he said at the door. "Right now Arthur and I have work to do."

I threw on my coat and gloves, not wanting them to argue. As much as I wanted them to get back together, when they were in the same room I felt an impending violence, or more accurate, a fragility or brittleness—even when they were civil, as they were now. Though it did not go away when we were alone, I liked them better by themselves.

My mother came out on the landing to wave us away. "Have a good time," she called.

"Where are we going?" I asked when we were on the interstate.

"Where do you think?" my father said.

"Not pizza."

My father laughed. "Nope."

"Then I don't know."

"What," my father asked, "do you want to do more than anything else in the world?"

"Drive," I said.

"That is exactly where we're going—to teach you how to drive."

"Why?"

"Why?" my father repeated, all innocence. "Because you don't know how to."

I was not really angry with him, and let it go.

"Arthur," my father said with a sigh. "Yes, your mother did call me. I'm glad she did."

"I am too," I said, calling a truce neither of us was foolish enough to trust. We were going up the hill and the Nova was losing speed. My father shifted into low. Behind us the city smoked in the bright cold.

"I'm moving," my father said. "Did your mother tell you?"

"No."

"Well, I am, to a new apartment starting next month. It's furnished and it has a kitchen."

"That's good," I said, but I wasn't thinking that. I did not know what it meant, only that they both should have told me earlier.

We came to the exit for the high school, and my father took it. We crossed the bridge and turned into the access road and drove until we reached the parking lot. It was empty, covered with a fresh coat of snow. Atop the hooded streetlamps perched gulls from the lake, flying sorties back and forth to the dumpsters. My father rolled to the center of the lot, turned off the car and held his keyring out to me. In his palm it rested like a dangerous insect.

"Are you ready?" he said, and I knew that for a while I would not be able to escape the girl and the kindness other people believed I needed. That was all right, I thought. Though in a sense both their sympathy and my grief were confused and would never connect, none of it was false. I would try not to question this gift.

Sunday they had a service for Annie's girl downtown at United Presbyterian, where the Van Dorns used to go. I had to wear my old suit, whose pants were floods. The church was overflowing. My mother promised we wouldn't stay long. I didn't know anyone there besides my father, and Annie, who sat in front where I couldn't really see her. While the priest talked on and on, I thought about how strange the connection between me and the girl and her mother was—a weird, secret triangle. My father followed us through the receiving line as if we were still a family. People stopped to hold Annie's and Mrs. Van Dorn's hands and say a few words. She was almost as I had remembered her—pretty, with her hair straight and bright against the black dress. My old crush on her returned, pumped through me like a drug. Waiting for my mother to get done, I thought of Lila and sobered.

Annie said she didn't recognize me. "With all the hair," she teased.

"I'm sorry," I said. I wondered if anyone had told

her it was me who'd found her, then thought probably not. It wouldn't make any difference to her.

"Thank you, Arthur."

"And you remember my husband Don," my mother said, reaching over me to touch his elbow.

"Of course, I couldn't forget Mr. Parkinson."

"We're all very sorry," my father said.

Outside there were TV cameras. We walked to the parking lot together, my mother and father in front, discussing Thanksgiving. In the car my mother said we were going to Pittsburgh. It did not feel like a victory.

Monday I met Lily and Lila at the bottom of the drive. I expected them to say something about me finding the girl, but we walked up the crunchy hump in single file, discussing how dumb it was for us to have to go to school on Friday. They were going to York to see their aunt who worked for Harley-Davidson. (No, Lily said, she didn't ride a bike.) They seemed unaware of the search. Maybe they didn't have a TV or read the *Eagle*. Maybe they weren't interested. I wanted to tell Lila alone to see if she'd console me, but that was impossible with Lily, and as we turned the curve into the woods and lost sight of Foxwood, I thought that it would be classier if she heard it from someone else. I also didn't tell Lila that I had missed her desperately all weekend or thought of us next summer in the back of the Country Squire at the Sky Vue Drive-In. Instead, we stood outside the gate, passing a cigarette between the three of us, and when the bus came I got on and headed for the rear.

In the corner Warren had tied his hood as tight as it would go. He rolled his eyes back and stuck out his tongue.

"You sick fuck," I said, and slid in and punched him in the arm so he'd stop.

"Did you have nightmares?"

"No," I said truthfully. "You?"

"One. I dreamed we had practice every day this week."

"That wasn't a dream."

"I said it was a nightmare. Hey, how come our names weren't in the paper? It just said 'two volunteers.' "

"That's us," I said, and sang the tagline of Jefferson Airplane's "Volunteers of America."

"Hey, Arty," Todd Johnson called from across the aisle. "Warren says you were pissing your pants."

"Not quite, Tojo," I said.

"Was she all gooped-up and nasty?" he asked, making a face. I noticed everyone around us had stopped talking. I thought I would enjoy this part of my celebrity, the recounting, but suddenly I didn't want to talk about it.

"No," I said, shrugging. "She was just drowned. I knew her mother when I was a little kid."

It was like that all day. By lunch I was tired of people coming over to me expecting some emotion. Eating my grilled cheese, I gazed up at the pats of butter stuck to the perforated ceiling. I shrugged and told them I had known Annie. They all seemed disappointed with me, as if I were being a spoilsport. I was glad when the bell rang and I could hide in music class.

We were bad in practice that week, as if—as Mr. Chervenick insisted—missing Friday had hurt us. We were giving up, he said; we had to question whether we had the desire to be a real band.

"Yeah," Warren said beside me, "a real bad one."

The snow came down all three days, and keeping my thirty-inch stride, I followed the contours of the tornado, peeking toward the footbridge, sure we would have another chance to find the girl, this time alive.

Neither Lila or Lily said a word about it. Wednesday when we saw the bus coming and quickly passed the butt around for last hits, I said I hoped they had a good time in York.

"What are you doing?" Lila asked, and I told her.

"You have fun too," she said.

"I will," I said, and on the bus scourged myself for saying something so dumb.

Warren could read me, and shook his head, smirking. He'd taken to calling her Delilah and snipping at my hair with his fingers.

"Don't say anything," I said. "Just shut up."

Thanksgiving it sleeted, and Armstrong stomped us, 48–6. Before the end of the first half we gathered in close formation behind the end zone, setting up for our show. If our team won we'd be eligible for the state tournament in Philadelphia, but we were down three TD's already. The stands were full of disappointed fans throwing small, hard erasers in the shape of the Liberty Bell. The sleet bled down our sheet music.

"This is it," Mr. Chervenick rallied us. "This is where you find out if you have what it takes."

Our drum major blew his whistle three times and we took the field. The stands were thinning, people going to the restrooms, the makeshift concession stands benefitting the PTA. The field was a mess, the grass between the hashmarks churned to a cold, gluey mud; the turf along the sidelines was untouched but icy. Our first rank of drummers had nearly made midfield when beside me Warren slipped and fell. In practice they trained us to ignore it when anyone screwed up so as not to draw attention to it, but I couldn't leave Warren in the mud. I stopped to give him my hand and the trombone following ran me down. I couldn't hear them through "Proud Mary" but I knew the people in the stands were laughing at us. I imagined Mr. Chervenick on the sidelines shaking his head in dismay, and for an instant couldn't get up. Warren pushed my hat at me, I grabbed my instrument, and we both ran through the formation to the pair of empty places. When the music allowed us a rest, I snuck a glance down at myself. My horn was smudged, a clump of turf clinging to the spit valve; my uniform was destroyed— and foolishly, for no reason, tears came to my eyes. I wasn't allowed to move, to break the symmetry of the brass, and by the time the chorus returned I was fine, worried that someone might have seen me. I'd say it was just sleet.

"That's all right, Arthur, Warren," Mr. Chervenick said as we came off. "Tough conditions."

"Fucking shit," Warren said.

"I know," Mr. Chervenick said. "Nothing you could do."

At home, when my mother pulled my uniform out of my gym bag, she said, "You fell down. Oh honey, are you all right?" She was already in her sleeveless blue dress for dinner but not made up.

"Why is it when anything happens you think I can't handle it?" I said. "I'm fine."

"Obviously you're not," she said, but glancingly, headed for the bathroom. We were not officially late yet, but she had begun to move through the furniture with a recklessness that I knew preceded leaving. "I'm going to have to soak this or it's not going to come clean. I'm sure no one's open today."

While she ran water in the tub I went to my room and sat on my bed. My clothes for dinner were laid out like armor. Dark slacks, white shirt. A striped tie my father used to help me with, standing behind me. I put on the pants and sat back down.

"Are you getting dressed?" she called, prodding.

"Yes," I said, lying flat on my back.

She looked in a few minutes later. "I'm going whether you come or not. There's leftover chicken in the fridge."

I pulled on the shirt and tucked it in, yanked the fuzzy gray socks on. My good shoes were too small and bit at my feet. I carried the tie like a snake.

"You look respectable!" my mother joked. She took the tie from me, made a loop and looked at it. "Okay," she said, "I think I remember this." Standing in front of me, she slid it around my neck, crossed it over and through and down. "Lift your chin." She pulled the knot tight and fixed the wings of my collar. All this time I was looking at her in her blue dress, thinking how beautifully strong her arms were, and how my father would look at her.

"You look pretty," I said.

"Thank you," she said. "We're going to be late."

We were. My grandparents and my aunt and my father were finishing their first drink in the living room. My father was in his suit, a smaller version of my grandfather, who I had never seen wearing anything else. My grandmother wore pearls, my aunt a cashmere sweater. The house was rich with the smell of gravy, and from the expensive stereo they kept beside the grandfather clock, a string quartet softly flowed. My mother, with her bare arms and blue heels, seemed too bright.

"Louise," my grandfather said, "what will you have?"

"Maybe," my mother said, pointing to his tumbler, "a wee scotch?" I noticed that both my aunt and grandmother were having white wine.

"Arthur?" He said it heartily, as if we were in business together. As if I had any choice but my usual ginger ale.

My mother sat by my father on the sofa, and I sat to one side. On the glass-topped table in front of us was a platter with crackers and a spreadable cheese, but the room was so neat that I didn't risk it.

"So," my aunt said, "how was Homecoming?"

"Good," I said. "We lost though."

"That's too bad."

"I fell down at halftime, right in the mud."

"Tell us," my grandmother said.

They all had another drink before we went into the dining room. The table was laid with water goblets and wine glasses, two different forks and spoons, a silver sugar bowl filled with cubes I used to snitch when I was a child. Beside my grandfather's chair stood a two-tiered cart from which he would serve us the turkey and mashed potatoes and stuffing and pea casserole and turnips and pearl onions in cream sauce. A covered gravy boat steamed from its blowhole; a cut-glass bowl of cranberry sauce waited at each end of the table. While my grandmother lit the candles and dimmed the lights we all stood behind our chairs, the places we had sat at every past Thanksgiving and Christmas. My father stood by my mother, ready to help her with her chair. I thought of Astrid because hers sat against the wall, empty. This year for the first time I would have elbow room. Otherwise there was no difference.

"Shall we?" my grandfather said, and we sat.

"Donald?" my grandmother said.

We bowed our heads.

I was pretty sure I did not believe in God—especially today—and this was a tricky part of the meal for me. Usually I made a point of not folding my hands or saying ''Amen'' at the end, but sometimes it was hard, with the silence, the grave faces of everyone I loved, not to feel guilty for it, slightly damned. Now as my father said grace as if nothing had changed, I listened to the list of things we were thankful for and made up my own. Lila. Warren. Astrid, who refused to talk with my father. My mother, whom, apparently, my grandparents had never liked. And, yes, my father, who I was now seeing for the third time in two months, and who I would not have been seeing if I hadn't discovered—by sheer luck—a dead child floating in a storm sewer. I knew no one would mention it tonight, and I thought of Annie and Mrs. Van Dorn having Thanksgiving somewhere. My mother had not had time to go over yet. I felt, looking around the table, that tonight we—my mother and I—belonged not here where we were no longer welcome but with them wherever they were. It was more of a wish than a prayer, flimsy.

''And most of all,'' my father said, ''we thank you for bringing us together.''

''Amen,'' we all said.

E I G H T

THE CAMERA CREWS COME in the middle of the day for the light, and Brock can't stop them. The Pittsburgh stations know to park farther on up the road, but every other day it seems like someone from Erie or Wheeling drives right up to the house. It's timing,

Brock thinks; the whole world is interested in the story because it's the holidays. He's seen Annie on TV, peeking from behind a curtain. The camera pans the snowy woods. They've quit watching the news, stopped delivery of the *Eagle*.

The state police come every day and take the same statement Annie's given them before, then walk around the pond, squatting when they spot a possible clue. They've questioned Brock twice and both times he's insisted he was at the mall, Christmas shopping. He shows them the bag of toys in his closet, and looking at the boxed Barbie he did in fact mean to give Tara, realizes the size of his lie, the smallness of his heart. The inspector seems to believe him, though each time he reminds Brock that they may question him again in the future. Brock asks about the TV people but the inspector says they can't do anything, the road's public property.

Annie has filed a restraining order against Glenn. After the memorial service he threatened her, said he had nothing to lose, that she'd taken everything from him. He wasn't drunk, just upset, making a fool of himself. Brock ended up having to manhandle him into the rented limousine in front of everyone. He keeps showing up as evening falls, drinking in his truck and shouting at the house.

"I shall pass through this furnace unscathed," he

bellows. "O Lord, restore the righteous and let judgment fall upon the wicked."

"You asshole," Annie screams from the steps, losing it, "leave me alone." Brock has come home to find her on the couch, exhausted, clutching her father's gun.

Brock calls and the township police come and roust Glenn, lock him up for the night. The next day he's there again, pious after a twelve-pack. He's quit his job, moved out of his parents' house. Annie thinks Brock should stay home from work.

He could do it. They have enough money. The mail brings checks from far-off states, singles sent by kids, change taped to index cards. While most of the notes are condolences, an anonymous few accuse both of them or Annie alone of killing Tara—and graphically, like a TV detective taking pleasure in laying out a murder. Several cranks, it seems to Brock, write the way Glenn talks. Her death is God's will, their shaky handwriting says, in payment for their sins. They compare Annie to Eve. What does that make him, Brock wonders. The postmarks are all different; some even sign their names. He can't believe so many different people say the same crazy things.

"Oh sure," the inspector says, adding them to his bulging manila envelope, "the hills are crawling with them."

But Brock doesn't want to stay home. He hates seeing Tara's room, the pink paint and the little quilt with hearts on it. He hasn't cried for her and it bothers him. He thinks he should grieve, but when he sees a commercial with Big Bird or a wisecracking child actor, all he feels is anger and then shame. She is dead, he reminds himself, she is gone and dead and never coming back. It's as if he refuses to believe it, but it's true; he's not going to run away from this one. At work the old people he takes care of are so insulated they treat him as if the accident never happened, and he likes that. He likes sharing lunch with Tricia and Neil Young, her laugh, the heaviness of her breasts. At home he'd have nothing to do. Though they've changed their number, the phone rings constantly; they unplug it, and then when they snap the plastic jack in to make a call, it goes off like a bomb. Daily, to escape, Annie visits her mother. They talk all afternoon; driving past her mother's place, Brock sees her car in the drive and knows he'll have to make dinner again. Hamburger Helper, tuna-noodle casserole. He's not allowed to be angry with her, he understands that. And he's not. Guilty himself, he's worried that as a mother Annie blames herself, and is withdrawing not only from him but the world. Her ankle is better, yet she hasn't returned to work. Nights she lies on the couch, gobbling Archway cookies and watching sitcoms. The laughtrack eats at Brock. She goes to bed early, and he's learned not to follow. She has pills she takes. Since Tara's been gone they haven't made love. He's talked to Tricia about it. He's even thought of calling Barb.

The Friday after Thanksgiving he gets his paycheck and stops on the way home to cash it, thinking he might buy a bottle of wine or two. It's a risk, but if it doesn't work out at least he'll put a good buzz on. He drops into a state store and picks up a pair of Almaden jugs, the Mountain Rhine she likes. It's snowing, and Brock props the bag on the seat so it won't roll around. If Glenn's there, he's ready. He keeps a prybar under the driver's seat; inch-thick, it'll snap a man's arm.

But when he gets home the road's empty. The day's just starting to fail; the water tower's lights snap on as he approaches. The Maverick is in the drive, plastic duct-taped over the broken window. It's not until he pulls in behind it that he sees the front door of the house is open and the hall is dark.

Brock runs across the yard and takes the front steps in two smooth bounds. The only light on is the one over the stove. There's a bloody lump of hamburger defrosting on a piece of foil.

"Annie?" Brock hollers, then runs for the bedroom. It's a mess, so is Tara's room, and next week

Child Protective Services is coming to see the house. Routine procedure, the inspector says, but to Brock it seems cruel. It was an accident. It was not Annie's fault.

She's not inside. Her boots are gone, her jacket, even her gloves. He closes the front door behind him and stands on the front porch. In the yard, garbage from the search has frozen into the snow. The barrel the police used for warmth still stands in the turn-around, blocking the back way to the pond.

Brock walks down the road under the blue glow of the water tower, looking for footprints. There are too many old ones. It's hard for him to believe so many people were here and none of them could do anything. She'll never forgive him for coming home late that day. He turns onto the back road, going through the woods now. He grew up in town with his aunt, and for him the stillness is a little creepy. Above, a squirrel chitters, working at a hard-won acorn. Brock doesn't know if Annie would do anything foolish. With her temper, she's capable. He passes the mound with its snow-covered fenceposts and follows the trail to the top of the hill, stands looking down.

She's there, below him, a black shape out in the middle of the pond. She's sitting on the ice, smoking, the glowing end a star in the dark. Brock is at once thankful and disheartened, weary of her suffering. He hates himself for this impatience. Like the searchers, he's helpless.

He waves but she's not looking up, and he picks his way down the hill. He stands on the bank, sure she can see him now. When she doesn't acknowledge him, he tests the ice with one foot. Near the bank it's soft and his toe goes through. He pulls back, dripping. With the light it's hard to tell what's solid.

"Annie," he calls.

She stubs the butt out, doesn't look up.

"Annie, come on."

He walks along the bank, testing, and when he finds a solid spot, steps gingerly onto the ice. It doesn't creak or give. With the weather lately it should be okay, he thinks hopefully. His rubber-soled workshoes aren't made for this. He baby-steps toward her, the dark outline slowly filling in. She's hunched over with her hands tucked into her armpits, squinting against the wind.

Brock sits down beside her on the ice. His pants stick to it.

"Aren't you cold?" he asks, joking.

Annie turns and looks at him, for the first time acknowledging his presence. She looks down at the ice, out at the woods. A flake catches in her eyelashes, and he remembers why he gave up everything he'd had with Barb for her.

"Do you know someone named Patricia Farr?"

Even in the cold Brock can feel his face fill with heat. The inspector, he thinks, damn him. "She's a girl at work."

"Were you screwing her when it happened?"

"She's fat," Brock says, as if it's proof of something, and is instantly ashamed. His aunt was right, he betrays everyone.

"At Susan's."

"I was buying Christmas presents."

"Was it the same room?" Annie asks. "Did you pour wine over her and do it in the tub too?"

"No," Brock says, but only because there is no other answer to the question. "Let's go inside."

"No," Annie says.

"I never said I'd stay."

"You can go now," she says. "You want to go. I want you to go."

After twenty minutes he stands and walks around. He's not dressed half as warmly as she is, yet the cold seems to have no effect. It's dark. The wind calls through the trees; on the highway traffic is dwindling. It's strange, Brock thinks, how he's no longer afraid of falling through.

One-thirty and Rafe has work tomorrow. He's hoping Glenn, who's been drinking steadily since he made bail, will pass out soon. Rafe paid again, but he doesn't mind. His parents left him money and the house; what else is he going to spend it on? Glenn's his friend, a fuck-up like him. No one else is going to help him.

They're sitting in the kitchen knocking back shots of Jack Daniel's, chasing them with Duke beer. Bomber's asleep upstairs. In the other room Eric Clapton leads Derek and the Dominos through "Bell Bottom Blues." Glenn's slurring and laughing at his own jokes, mumbling his religious shit. Rafe is just keeping him company, drinking one to Glenn's two, watching the clock. The table is sticky and littered with cigarette butts and peanut shells, the Sunday want ads. Several times Glenn has knocked over the shot-glass. A few hours ago they thought about dinner; now Glenn's hungry.

"We're going to need something to puke," he says. "The Burger Hut serves till eleven."

"Glenn-man, it is one-thirty in the morning. There's no one open, man."

"Fuck that."

I don't want to fade away, Clapton sings. *Give me one more day please.*

Rafe goes to the cupboard. "We've got soup. Tomato, chicken noodle?"

"Soup," Glenn says. "I want something to eat-eat, not some fucking soup. Did you ever puke noodles?"

"That's all we've got."

"What did Jesus feed the multitudes with?" He'll break into pointless parables like this; it drives Rafe crazy. Even worse is when he drops to his knees in the middle of the room. Rafe understands that his head is messed up from Tara and watches him for signs that he might try to kill himself again. Sometimes Glenn mentions that he needs to refill his prescription, but Rafe has never seen him take his pills. He doesn't know where Glenn goes during the day. Earlier this week he came home and Glenn was sitting where he is now, drenched from head to toe, his clothes dripping, boots covered with mud. When he asked what happened, Glenn said he tried to go home but they didn't want him. He wouldn't explain any further, and Rafe saw a blankness in his eyes that told him not to push it. Glenn needs time, Rafe thinks, like he needed time after his own mother died.

"Fish, I don't know, man. We don't have any."

"Fuck it," Glenn says, "I'm not hungry." He lays his head on his arms.

I don't want to fade away, Clapton pleads.

"Come on, man, let's get you to bed."

"One more," Glenn says. He lifts his head and pours a shot which overflows. The whiskey darkens the want ads. "Are you going to drink with me?"

"I've got work in the morning."

"You're drinking with me. Here." He gets up shakily and totters over to Rafe, spilling as he goes.

"Watch what you're doing, man."

Glenn looks down. "Sorry, man. It's just a fucking floor."

"It's my mother's floor."

"I'm sorry, all right?" Glenn takes the want ads from the table and swabs at the spilled whiskey. "All right. Let's drink. Here." He gives Rafe the nearly empty glass, takes the bottle by the neck and tips it up. Rafe watches his Adam's apple bob; there's only an inch or so left and Glenn's going to finish it. Rafe wants to take the bottle from him but doesn't. It's easier.

Glenn drains it and whacks it down on the counter. "Dead motherfucking soldier."

"All right, man, time to crash." Rafe turns him with a hand and steers him toward the door. Glenn weaves, lurches as if the whiskey has just now caught up to him and thumps his head against the doorframe. It knocks him back a step, into Rafe's arms.

Glenn laughs. "That feels pretty good," he says, and before Rafe can stop him, he grabs hold of the jamb, rears back and rams his forehead into it, butts it like a hammer driving a nail. It's not a joke; he's not stopping. Upstairs Bomber barks a warning.

Rafe wrestles Glenn into the hall and, tangled, they crash to the floor. Glenn doesn't fight back. Pinned, he looks up at Rafe, a drop of blood running down into his eyebrow.

"Glenn-man, what are you doing?"

"I don't know," Glenn says, smiling, honestly puzzled. "What am I doing?"

"Man," Rafe says, heaving from the tussle, "man," but doesn't know what to say. "You can't do this, man."

May makes Tara's bed, tucking the quilt under the child-sized flannelette pillow, sitting Winnie-the-Pooh to one side, her big bunny the other. Bun-bun. She goes to the bookshelf and straightens the spines. *Goodnight, Moon, Curious George, Where the Wild Things Are.* May opens one by Dr. Seuss and leafs through it, surprised she still knows the words.

Look what we found
In the park
in the dark.
We will take him home.
We will call him Clark.
He will live at our house.
He will grow and grow.
Will our mother like this?
We don't know.

May fits it back into the shelf. She doesn't have time for this. The lady from Child Protective Services will be here in twenty minutes. May wouldn't have known if Brock hadn't called her. Annie doesn't seem to care. She sees the visit as an insult and refuses to do anything. All morning May scrubbed the kitchen and the bathrooms while Brock vacuumed. It was a shock; May had never considered him responsible before. He's had his hair cut just for this, and is wearing corduroys and a nice shirt. Together they conspired to send Annie to the store for milk and fresh vegetables to make the refrigerator look full. She seemed glad to go. She's just gotten back and is downstairs, sitting on the couch watching her soap opera. May wishes she would wear something other than her jeans—a pant-suit, anything—and maybe put on some makeup. These people are serious.

"What are they going to do to me?" Annie asked

her earlier, and May couldn't answer. It does seem foolish; Tara is gone. May is angry too, but she can't let anything more happen to Annie.

May hefts the laundry basket and sets it on the floor by Tara's dresser, starts putting away the clothes she washed at her place. Tiny socks and undershirts, frilly panties, tights, overalls, turtlenecks, sweatshirts. Some are presents May herself hunted down at the mall. She recognizes gifts from her birthday, from last Christmas. They'll all end up in Goodwill, she thinks. She lines up the shoes in the closet, straightens the dresses on their hangers. Done, she stands at the door holding the empty basket, looking in. It really is a nice room for a child. She remembers Annie and Glenn painting the walls and laying the carpet. May lent them the crib Charles made for Raymond, in which Dennis and then Annie slept. That was less than four years ago, May thinks. What happened?

"Here she comes," Brock hollers from downstairs.

"She's early," May complains, then hustles down with the basket. It's hers and there's nowhere to put it. She thought she'd have time to stick it in her car.

Outside the woman is swinging into the drive. A big, black Galaxie 500 with white, official writing too small to read on the door. Brock takes the basket from May and thunders up the stairs.

Annie grudgingly turns off the TV, as if this has nothing to do with her.

"Try to be polite," May says.

Annie walks past her to the door and opens it, waits for the woman to cross the lawn. May doesn't know her. She's dark-haired and young, in her early thirties, with a perm, an expensive calf-length wool coat and a massive black handbag. She's carrying a brown accordion folder, and when she reaches the porch May can see her gloves are real leather, creased at the knuckles. When she says hello she holds the *o* too long. Pittsburgh, May thinks, probably went to college.

Her name is Sharon. She takes her gloves off to greet them. A single silver band, elegant. Brock introduces himself without saying what relation he is to Annie. He takes her coat and hangs it in the closet. Underneath she's wearing a mustard top and a black skirt, dark hose and smart kneeboots. Beside her Annie looks terrible.

"For now I'll only need to talk to you," Sharon says, and Annie leads her into the kitchen. May follows, asking if Sharon wants some coffee. She says yes, that would be wonderful. May thinks that her plan is working. She has baked a plate of cookies, and sets it on the table between them. She waits for the coffee, eavesdropping.

Sharon opens her folder and starts filling out forms, asking Annie simple questions. May has told Annie not to smoke, so immediately she has to light up, waving the cigarette around, dismissing each answer. May knows the tone; Annie's already lost interest. Concentrating on her paperwork, Sharon doesn't seem to notice.

"Officially," Annie says, "we're still married. Five years in August."

"And your daughter's name?"

"Tara. Tara Elizabeth." May detects a change, a hardness in this.

"Date of birth?"

May knows all the answers.

"Okay," Sharon says, finishing a sheet. "Good." She tears it along a perforation, sets both pieces aside.

The coffee's ready but May doesn't want to leave. She stands at the counter with her back to the table, waiting for them to go on.

"Mrs. Van Dorn?" Sharon asks. "I'm afraid the rest of the interview is confidential, if you don't mind."

"No," May says, "I was just going to pour."

Annie gets up. "Go ahead, Ma." She takes the mugs from her, holds the lid down while she tips the pot.

May still hasn't moved.

"I'll be all right," Annie says, and May can see that it's true, that she's not going to let this woman hurt her.

"I'll be in the living room," May says, but even as she's leaving, she hesitates, looks back as if Annie might need her.

Annie's first day back at work is Sunday brunch. It's an easy shift, a buffet. All she has to do is keep track of drink orders, take an occasional chafing dish of sausages to the skirted table. Families come in their church clothes, the girls dolled up in gauzy sleeves, boys in velvet breeches. Annie leans down to hear them ask for cranberry juice and Cokes.

"What do you say?" the mothers prompt.

"Please."

At the bar Annie arranges the glasses around her tray according to the table: mimosa, white wine, screwdriver, mimosa, Coke, beer, mimosa, bloody, bloody. It's been a while, and she makes mistakes, apologizing as she switches drinks. If Barb were here she'd tease Annie, but the other girls ignore it. In the break room they don't know what to say except that they're sorry, that they're glad she's back. Annie knows they're just worried. They don't mean to hurt her.

Out on the floor she can feel the club members gauging her, wondering why she isn't at home, what they would do if something like this happened to them. One older woman she's served for months at a corner table holds on to her wrist and says, "I wish there was something I could say."

"Thank you," Annie says, to get her to let go.

It's not all bad. She's busy. The crowd is constant, another rush around one-thirty. Annie wills herself into the rhythm of prepping, serving, bussing, then prepping again. It's not like the house, where she can't think of anything else. Only once in a while does she stop and—tricked by routine—think of Tara waiting to be picked up at her mother's.

At break she smokes a cigarette by herself on the loading dock, arms folded over her breasts against the cold. The bottom of the parking lot is empty and snow-covered; beyond, a fairway stretches like a white avenue through the trees. A car passes on the road, and she thinks of the Sundays Barb stood here puffing while she and Brock were at Susan's. He's going to leave her as soon as she's strong enough; they both know it. In his eyes, half the battle's over; Child Protective Services has cleared her. He'll never know what it means to be a parent, she thinks. He's being polite, not fighting with her, trying to be nice. Annie can't remember what she saw in him. A fuck. She smokes the Marlboro down to the writing and flicks it off the dock, watches it poke a hole in the snow. She's not strong enough, Annie thinks, she may never be. He can leave. He will anyway. Inside, in the bathroom, she chews a stick of gum while she fixes her hair and is ready to face her audience again.

She hasn't had time to take the Maverick in. Going home, the plastic bulges in the window, shouldering her. Even with the heat up, the car's freezing. She's got to start worrying about all these little things again. It exhausts her just thinking about it. She imagines letting the car drift into the oncoming bridge abutment. She could fold her hands in her lap, close her eyes and step on the gas pedal. But she doesn't. The bridge with its teenage graffiti—"Joann I love U 4ever Dave"—passes overhead. She's started to think about dinner.

When she gets home, Brock is making barbecued chicken and stuffing from a box. The Steelers have won again. Three empty beer bottles sit on the coffee table—unsubtle proof that he wasn't at Susan's with his Patricia. It's pointless; the inspector says they do it at lunch. He's shown her the girl's picture. She has a double chin and frizzy hair. Annie doesn't understand.

"How was work?" Brock asks.

"Good," Annie says.

"Are you going in tomorrow?"

"I said I was."

"I didn't know how you'd feel after today."

"I feel tired," Annie says, plopping down on the couch. "I feel like I've done something."

"Good," Brock says, overly cheerful. He comes in wearing an oven mitt, clutching a meat fork. "That's great."

"Please," Annie says, "will you cut the crap and start acting like a normal human being?"

She can see Brock wants to explode all over her but can't. She doesn't know which is more offensive, him pitying her or pretending nothing has happened.

She works the full week on day shift, getting home in time to make dinner. She reads the mail, writes thank-yous to people who have sent checks. Saturday while the Maverick is being fixed, Brock takes her and her mother Christmas shopping. There are two weeks left and the mall is jammed. She sees children everywhere, hears their squeals coming from the video arcade. She ignores the people pointing. Only the line for Santa Claus bothers her. In it waits a girl wearing Tara's coat. They have to stop and turn around, give Annie a minute in the Potato Patch.

"Maybe we should go," her mother says to Brock. "Maybe this wasn't such a good idea."

"I'll be okay," Annie says, "I just need something to eat."

Her mother raves over the tacos, but they don't go back past the North Pole. It's good, Annie thinks, that she has limits. In a way, she doesn't want to lose this part of Tara too easily.

On her day off, she visits the cemetery, pulling her car off the road and walking back in through the stones. Her mother owns plots for all of them—herself, Annie, Raymond and Dennis—though she doesn't expect they'll use them. Tara is beside Annie's father. Cemented into the ground in front of his grave is a vase. Annie thought of getting one for Tara until she conferred with her mother.

"A windy day," her mother said, "forget it," and it's true, even a breeze plucks the flowers right out, sends the bright heads tumbling. Annie brings them anyway, packing snow around the stems with her fingers. She has seen other people visiting alone talking to their loved ones—old Polish women mostly—but she does not feel close to Tara or her father here, rather the opposite. With her father, she accepts this distance, accepts the fact that time has passed.

Hot August he used to take her fishing out at the

new lake. He had a glazed ceramic jar with a lid she'd made for him in art in which he'd grind out his Lucky Strikes. When the jar was full they'd call it a day. She has pictures stuck in her mirror of herself standing on the concrete launch, holding a stringer of perch, crappie, a lucky trout. Just her—her brothers were too old for that. "The hell with them," her father used to say, lounging on the cooler, an orange life preserver behind his head. "They wouldn't know a good time if it bit them square in the behind."

Annie refused to visit him in the hospital; on the phone she said she'd see him when he got home.

"Don't wait for me too long," he said, his voice rags.

"Do you want me to come in?" she asked.

"I think you'd better."

"Did you hear that?" her mother said from the kitchen extension.

"I heard it!"

"I don't want you two fighting," her father said, so they fought in the car.

Squatting there in the cold, Annie misses him only dimly. She misses holding Tara, brushing her hair, feeling for a new tooth pushing through. She doesn't need a stone to remember her.

Her mother comes with her sometimes, and sometimes goes alone. Annie finds her footprints, and a man's which she assumes are Glenn's. She hasn't run into him since he was arrested the second time. Inwardly, Annie worries that he may try something after Brock leaves. She keeps the gun loaded.

His father has called, saying Glenn's distraught, that he doesn't know what he's doing. Annie has always liked Frank Marchand, but he's wrong; Glenn's sick. Whether it's just depression or a real mental illness, he's sick and possibly dangerous and she's not taking any chances.

"In your position," Glenn's father concedes, "I suppose you don't have a choice."

When she's not working and Brock is, she stays out of the house, spends time with her mother. Her mother thinks they should move in with her. It's foolish, two houses. Annie doesn't tell her that any day Brock is going to take off; it would give her more ammunition. They drink coffee and play gin and talk about the Parkinsons filing for divorce.

"Twenty-three years," her mother says.

"They always seemed happy to me," Annie says, discarding. Her mother lets her smoke in the house now, as if they've come to an understanding.

"The new people are nice."

"Where are they from?" Annie asks, to keep the conversation alive. The afternoon deepens, the windows dim. She keeps an eye on the clock above the fridge, waits until it's safe to go home. Her mother walks her to the door and, in yet another new ritual, gives her a hug. She stands there while Annie backs out, waving in the cold.

The road's empty, the flag of the mailbox up. One from Bradford, Kane, Altoona. Lately the number has been dwindling, and Annie's glad. She has twenty minutes until Brock gets home, and before taking her coat and boots off, sticks a pot of water on. She finds a jar of sauce in the cupboard, a box of spaghetti with the end taped shut. Bread, butter. She turns the early news on to fill the house, then stands at the stove, customizing the sauce with spices. The floor is freezing and she gives the pot a good stir before going upstairs to get her slippers.

She is sitting on the end of her bed putting them on when she notices the room is different. It's subtle, a subtraction of something not there in the first place. Brock's stereo—it's missing. She goes to the closet; his smaller half is empty, the pole bare of hangers. He's forgotten his toothbrush, probably on purpose. His razors and shaving cream are gone, his nail clippers. Annie checks his dresser drawers. Cleaned out.

She knew he would leave, but now that he has it's no consolation. He could have at least told her. But that wouldn't be Brock.

Downstairs the sauce is bubbling, spewing like a geyser. The stove is a mess. She turns it off and sits down at the table and finds she's carrying the toothbrush. In the other room the news is going on and on. She gets up, goes to the front door, opens it and throws the toothbrush into the yard. It skitters to a stop. She slams the door and turns off the news and sits on the couch. She lies down and looks at the sky in the front window. Cold gray. At least the waiting's over, she thinks. Now what?

An hour later she is still lying there watching the sky darken when she hears a car on the road. The sound jerks her head off the cushion. It wouldn't be him. She thinks of Glenn and the gun upstairs and dashes across the room to the window. Before she sees it, she recognizes the engine, a high-pitched metallic ringing that reminds her of a wind-up toy.

The yellow Bug comes into view and Annie runs outside in her slippers. Barb swings in behind her car.

"He called and told me," Barb says. She shows Annie the bag with the bottle in it and they embrace.

"I'm sorry," they both say.

"Jinx."

"I owe you a Coke," Annie says, but can't keep from blubbering.

"Turn it off," Barb says, just beginning herself.

In the town where Glenn's fathers were born, there was a square with benches and swings and seesaws. Which one took him there he can't remember. It's not in any of his pictures; Glenn has to draw it in. He wakes late in the day and sits in his long underwear at the dining room table, laboring over a sketchpad with his colored pencils. He gets things out of perspective and proportion but it's unimportant. He can see the streets, the dust in summer. The store his father robbed has two gas pumps out front with glass heads; you can watch the amber juice bubble. Glenn hasn't tried to draw his father. He envisions him in prison, playing solitaire, his face the same as Glenn's, and thinks that finally he understands him, that the blood they share is a stronger bond than he used to believe.

He only shows Rafe the town and the portraits of Tara he's copied from photos. The pictures of the old house and Annie he keeps flat under his mattress; when he takes them out when he's alone, they're smudged, the red lead staining the boxspring's ticking. He remembers her opening to him, and thinks of Brock. He can't go by the house anymore or the judge will give him time. "You're a young man," he said before suspending Glenn's sentence. "If I were you I would cut my losses and move on to the next part of my life.''

Glenn's driven past the road, watching for Brock's car. He knows that Annie's back on nights, which means she and Barb have patched things up. Deep in the morning, when he wakes to take a piss, he thinks of her alone in the house, asleep, her father's revolver on the night table by her head. He thinks of Tara's room and the snow blowing over her grave. His truck is outside; Bomber's asleep on a pile of dirty clothes. Glenn gets into the warm bed and lies on his back, open-eyed.

''I wish you would tell me what to do,'' he prays.

Late the next afternoon, as he's working on Tara's chin, he suddenly stops and puts down his pencil. The photo is from the mall package, the last pictures they have of her. He's never given Annie or her mother a set. He takes two of each print—the wallets, the five-by-sevens and eight-by-tens—and fits them into an envelope.

In the truck he decides it's not enough, pulls a U-turn and heads for the mall. It takes him a while to find a store that sells frames. He only has enough money for one of the nicer large ones, and he needs two. He asks the cashier if they take checks.

''All major credit cards,'' she offers.

''I don't have any of those,'' Glenn says.

A line is piling up behind him.

"I can hold them for you." The cashier moves to take the frames, but Glenn says, "That's all right," and picks them off the counter and walks out of the store.

"Sir," he hears her call, "sir!" but he's running, dodging the shuffling holiday shoppers. It's funny how they part to let him through. It makes Glenn laugh.

Annie is bringing in a busbox of fruit cups and saucers when Barb says she has a phone call. She swings the box off her shoulder and down to the counter where Mark the dishwasher begins emptying it, cramming the untouched melon balls and strawberry halves into the Insinkerator with his bandaged hands. She wipes her own on her apron before taking the phone.

"Glenn was just here," her mother says. "I thought I should warn you."

"Are you all right?"

"I'm fine. He brought over those pictures he had taken, do you remember those?"

Annie doesn't.

"Of Tara," her mother explains reluctantly. "They're very nice. He's had one framed or framed it himself, I'm not sure. I told him I could take a set for you, but he didn't want to leave them with me.''

"Did you call the police?"

"He was very polite. He even had a cup of tea."

"So you didn't call them."

"I did," her mother says. "I thought you'd want me to."

"Good."

"I don't know what you think they're going to do."

"I don't know either," Annie says, "but I'm glad you called them."

Barb says she can stay at her place tonight if she doesn't mind sharing a bed. It's a joke; in a way they already have. Thank God for Barb.

Work sucks. Annie gets a cracked busbox and the oil from the Caesar salad leaves a line on her shoulder. The special tonight is Maine lobster; she hates the juice and roe, the red carcasses, the scratchy legs. Mark the dishwasher feeds them into the Insinkerator, covers the hole with a plate so bits of shell don't fly out like shrapnel. They serve dessert, and while their customers linger over Irish coffees, take a ten-minute break.

Annie and Barb go down to the loading dock for a cigarette. It's so cold they can't smell the dumpster, and clear, the snow on the fairway starlit. The spotlight stripes the interiors of parked cars with shadows. Even in January they've seen people doing it in backseats. They search a stack of milk crates for clean ones, turn two over and sit.

"Why don't you move in with me?" Barb says, continuing a day-old conversation.

"That's nice," Annie says. "I don't think I'm ready to leave the house yet. It's weird."

"No, it's not." She blows a smoke ring, pokes it with her Marlboro. "I don't know; I think your mom's right, you'd be safer."

"Yeah," Annie says, but not in agreement, more as a signal that she doesn't want to talk about it.

A truck glides down the road, the sound of its engine trailing behind a second. It turns between the lamp-tipped pillars of the club entrance and crosses the causeway beside ten's water hazard.

"He wouldn't come here," Annie says, but stands. They're both protected by the shadow of the doorway.

Barb touches her arm. "Maybe he won't see us. It's probably not even him."

"It's him."

The headlights reach the black edge of the clubhouse and disappear.

"Would he know to come back here?" Barb asks. She's standing now.

"My car's right there."

"Let's go inside."

"No," Annie says. "I'm sick of this shit."

"I'll go call the cops."

"No, stay here with me. I want you to be a witness."

The truck reappears at the far end of the lot, creeping along. It's his. Annie steps to the rubberized edge of the dock, into the light. He brakes at her car, then keeps going. Maybe he's seen her. If he has a gun, she's dead. Fuck him.

"Hey!" she shouts, waving her arms over her head as if to flag down a train. "Fuck you!"

The truck turns the corner and faces them, the headlights blinding. She can see the shaggy outline of Bomber in the passenger seat. The truck stops short of the dock, sits there chugging. White exhaust pours up behind the bed.

"This is stupid," Barb says.

The door opens and Glenn steps out. He's carrying a package, probably the pictures her mother was talking about. "Annie."

"You're not supposed to be here," she says. "Legally you're not allowed within a hundred yards of me."

"I've brought you some pictures of Tara. Your

mother said you'd like them." He walks toward the dock with the package out in front of him, gingerly, as if she's holding a gun on him.

"I don't want them," Annie says.

"They're pictures of Tara."

"I said I don't want them."

"I'll just leave them here." He reaches the dock and lays the package at her feet, starts to back away.

"Why don't you listen to me?" Annie says. "I don't want them. I don't want anything from you." She picks the package up—it's heavier than she thought—and flings it at him. It lands with a crunch.

Glenn stops walking backwards and looks at her.

"Let's go inside," Barb says, and grabs her arm.

"That is our daughter," Glenn says, pointing to Annie. "That is our blood you're throwing on the ground." He turns and walks toward the truck.

Annie runs down the stairs of the loading dock, scoops up the package and charges after Glenn. He's halfway in when she catches him. She throws the package at him and follows it with her fists, screaming, "You fucker!" The horn goes off. Glenn pushes her away, but she's on him again, digging her nails into his face. Bomber is pulling at Glenn's arm, growling, Glenn shouting for him to get off. Behind her, Barb is screaming, and then Annie's head is suddenly numb and she's flying backwards out of the cab and falling hard in the snow. He has shot her, she thinks, unsure. Heat swarms to her face, fills and overflows.

Glenn is standing over her. "I'm sorry," he keeps saying, holding a hand to his head and turning around as if looking for help.

"You better get your ass out of here," Barb threatens from the loading dock. "You better just leave right the fuck now."

"Are you all right?" Glenn asks Annie.

She can't feel her nose or her teeth, only a runniness. Something's broken. She tries her arms and finds they still work, sits herself up. There's blood on her uniform.

"You're going to jail," Annie says.

Barb calls Annie's mother and takes her to the emergency room. Her nose isn't broken, only some stitches in her mouth, a loose tooth. She'll have to stick to a soft diet for a while.

"You say your ex-husband did this?" the nurse says.

"Husband," Annie says, and has to go through another form with a policeman. Yes, she wants to file charges; no, she's not sure where his residence is.

"Did you see him do it?" Annie asks Barb in the car.

"Not really. You just kind of dropped all of a sudden."

"Then he only hit me once."

"Once was enough," Barb says.

"We should have gone inside."

"Shit," Barb says, "I wasn't going to say anything."

The next morning she wakes up and her lips are crusted. Barb is asleep on the couch downstairs. It hurts to chew the banana she has for breakfast. It hurts to drink anything. Smoking's okay; it stings a little inhaling.

"I always thought he was an asshole," Barb says.

"He wasn't then," Annie says. "He turned into one. I don't know what happened."

"You're being generous when there's no reason to be."

They're watching "Let's Make a Deal" when Annie remembers all of his shit in boxes in the basement. She and Barb lug them upstairs and outside, pile them neatly in the snow at the end of the drive. She calls Glenn's father.

"Are you all right?" he asks. "The police told us what happened. They can't find him."

"Then you don't know where he is."

"Rafe said he took off sometime last night."

"Well, I've got a bunch of his stuff I can't keep anymore, and it's going to get snowed on if somebody doesn't come pick it up."

"I can come over," his father says. "I'm very sorry about everything, we both are."

"I know you are," Annie says.

When he does arrive, she watches him from the window. He opens the trunk and the back doors and slowly fills the big Plymouth, from time to time glancing at the house. He seems older since she last saw him, resting a heavy box on the bumper before jerking it up and into the trunk. Halfway through the stack he's red-faced and puffing. She's sorry; it's not his fault. She'd like to help him. She hopes Frank understands that she can't.

$N I N E$

DR. BRADY'S OFFICE was downtown, above the Hot Dog Shoppe. You had to enter the restaurant and take a left through another door, where there were mailboxes at the bottom of a steep and darkly shellacked staircase. The linoleum was old and bumpy underfoot.

Around the rail at the top stood six closed doors, numbered plainly, as in a dream. The building was old, and as Dr. Brady brought up and I downplayed my problems, we could hear rising from the heating grate the mingled conversations and clashing dishes of the Shoppe's patrons. From working at the Burger Hut I had learned not to trust food prepared by anyone other than myself, but the smell of grilling onions that leaked up through the floorboards tempted me, and after our session I would rumble down the stairs and scarf two chili dogs with onions and cheese.

The divorce was uncontested, legal a week after it was filed by my mother. My father was not living with another woman, but told me he was seeing one. He wanted to be honest with me, and between driving figure eights in reverse and parallel parking, he said my mother knew about her. He seemed solemn and apologetic, yet proud, as if he half resented asking my blessing.

"Has she told you anything?" he asked.

"No," I said, not really wanting to know.

"Her name is Marcia Dolan and she works at the new Mellon Bank downtown. She has two girls, both a good deal younger than you." He paused as if he wanted an answer from me, as if I knew who this woman was or had any opinion of her.

"Okay," I said.

"Maybe we could have dinner sometime, the three of us."

"Sure."

Dr. Brady was interested in why I said yes.

"I said 'sure,' " I corrected him. "It's different."

"Then what exactly were you communicating to your father there?"

He didn't have to tell me I was unhappy with the situation. Everyone involved knew that. My mother's hope was that he could tell her why finding the girl didn't seem to bother me. Halfway through the session, his questions turned to the search, and I had to go over it step by step, substituting a cigarette for the roach.

"And when you saw her," he asked, "how did that make you feel?"

"Afraid," I said.

"Why?"

"She was dead," I explained patiently.

I had to gobble the two dogs before my mother came to get me, and riding home in the Country Squire, felt them bubbling in my gut.

"Did you have a good session?" she asked.

"I guess," I said.

"What did you talk about today?"

"The same stuff as always."

My mother sighed, tired of my indifference. "I

know you don't like to go, but I think you need to. I can't get you to talk with me about these things.''

"Like what," I said, "Dad's girlfriend?"

"Like why you're high all the time and don't seem to care about anyone but yourself.''

"Fuck that," I said—just a sullen mumble—and she hit me. She flung a backhand across the front seat and caught me on the forehead.

"You don't talk to me like that.''

I turned to the window, defiant, viciously proud that I wasn't crying.

"I'm sorry," she said sternly, not apologizing, and started using how bad her day had been as an excuse.

I sat there pretending not to listen. Outside, drifted snowfences protected the white fields. I was going to win this one, and knowing that let me forgive her. I really shouldn't have said it. I could have said worse things. I could have asked about her lover. ("And why didn't you?" Dr. Brady would say.) It was a pretty good shot, I thought. She hadn't even looked, just lashed her arm out and whacked me.

That night Astrid called. When I got on she asked if everything was all right.

"What do you mean 'everything'?" I asked. We hadn't talked since I had found the girl.

"I mean you. Are you all right?''

"Yes," I said, mindful of my mother on the couch.

"Mom says she hit you in the face."

"Yeah."

"She's really upset about it."

"Right," I answered, as if waiting for her point.

"So will you tell her you're okay? She's flipping out. This is new to her. She never hit either of us before. Dad never hit us."

"I know."

"So tell her you're okay, all right? Christ, every time I call it's something new. She thinks you're flipping out about Annie's girl."

"Not me," I said.

"Is that right or are you just saying that? That's what she's worried about."

"I'm fine."

"If you are, then fine; if you're not, pretend you are and make her believe it."

"I am," I said, a little hard, and my mother glanced over.

"Because if you can just hang on I will be back there in four months, but if this shit keeps up I'm going to have to take hardship leave, and I do not want to do that."

"I wouldn't want you to have to do that," I taunted.

"All right," Astrid said, "okay. Now how was Thanksgiving?"

In music and at practice after school, Warren and I bore the ridicule of our bandmates with studied apathy. The Mud Brothers, they called us, but only until the next game, when one of the smaller girl clarinetists went down spectacularly, breaking her wrist. Mr. Chervenick was psyching us up for the final home game in two weeks. It was scheduled, he kept reminding us, the day after Beethoven's birthday, and we were working on the opening of the Fifth Symphony. Dit-dit-dit-daaa. From there we would segue into "Fanfare for the Common Man," a favorite with both the brass and the percussion. Since the summer the band had improved musically, Mr. Chervenick said, but the tornado was a joke. He was like a coach dressing us down after a sloppy game.

"Just once before I die," he said from his little podium, "I would like to see it done right. I don't think you are the group that is going to do it. I would be very surprised if you were. I think you're capable of it. Anyone is capable of it. Any one hundred and twenty-two students from this school are capable of making the tornado, but you have to want to do it. You have to want it with everything inside you. Every single one of you has to say to yourself, 'I am going to make this happen. Me.' Nobody else is going to do this for you. I know, I know, the football team lost its chance, but we still have ours. So are we going to be like them and blow it?''

"No!'' everyone yelled. I decided I liked him when he got himself worked up.

"Or are we going to be the ones who finally do it right?''

"Yes!''

"Do we have what it takes inside?''

Warren tapped me. "What the hell is he talking about?''

I shrugged and bellowed, "Yes!''

Between practice and seeing Dr. Brady I only rode home with Lila once a week. I had seen her without her glasses. We were walking uphill in the cold when she stopped and took them off to wipe the fog from her lenses. She did not suddenly become beautiful, only more vulnerable, squinting like someone who's just woken up. I daydreamed of inviting her over Friday night when my mother was out drinking with her friends: we would get stoned and watch TV with the lights out like all those couples in the commercials, except no one would interrupt us. Mornings, when we met at the bottom of the hill, we greeted each other formally, saying, "Lila,'' "Arthur,'' and alone in bed I'd hear her voice saying my name and imagine the two of us in the living room under my mother's afghan, our clothes strewn over the floor.

I did not tell Dr. Brady any of this.

I shouldn't have told Warren.

"She's a mess," he said. "I don't know what you're thinking, man."

"I'm not thinking," I said. "This isn't something you can think about."

"Hey, don't jump all over me. Ask her out or something."

"I will."

"Yeah right," he said.

Two days later, Lila was waiting for me at the bottom of our stairs, alone.

"Hi," I said, startled.

"Hey," she said.

Lily was sick with the flu.

"Which means I'm going to get it next," Lila said.

We walked along the road and into the woods. The drive had been spread with cinders and we crunched as we headed uphill. A pickup came up behind us and I followed Lila off to the left, stood on the crumbling edge of the road while the truck passed. Trudging up the hump again, neither of us said a thing, as if we needed Lily to speak to each other.

Finally I stopped. We were halfway up, in the middle of the woods. Lila went on a few steps and stopped, looking back at me.

"Want to split a cigarette?" I asked.

"Okay." She came back warily.

I handed it to her after the first hit, careful not to lip it. I put my hands in my pockets and blew out a cloud.

"What do you say we blow off school today?" I said.

"And do what?"

"I don't know, hang around."

"Where?"

"Here."

"I've got things I've got to do," Lila said. "You know I don't get stoned."

"We don't have to get stoned," I said, but defensively; the moment had passed.

"You've got practice you can't miss." She pointed the cigarette at my case as if it were incriminating.

"Yeah. It was a dumb idea."

She didn't contradict me, just passed the cigarette back.

"You know what I'd like to see," Lila said, as if we'd been discussing movies. *"The Godfather, Part Two."*

"Yeah," I said bitterly, disconsolate, "it's downtown."

"It's supposed to be really good but really violent."

"That's what the paper said."

"Your friend Warren said you might want to see it with me."

I thought, simultaneously, that it was none of his business and that I could never repay him enough.

"He did," I said, reeling. "Yes, I would. If you want to. It's supposed to be really good."

"I'd like to." Lila took the cigarette from my hand, took a last drag and flicked it high out over the snow. She turned and started walking again. I thought I should have tried to kiss her, and rushed to catch up.

"When?" I asked, completely at her mercy.

I caught Warren in the parking lot. I wrapped my arms around him from behind and lifted him off the ground.

"I knew you'd never ask her," he explained.

"Not true," I said, "that is un-fucking-true," and like a hero told him the whole story.

"I don't know her family," my mother admitted, slightly concerned that Lila was from Foxwood. "I'm sure she's very nice." She thought it was wonderful but said until I got my permit I would not be allowed to drive her car. My father agreed.

"So who do you want to chauffeur you two on Saturday?" she said.

It was not a hard decision. I could clean our car; my aunt's old Nova was hopeless. My mother promised not to peek at us in the mirror.

After the slapping incident we had reached another trucc. I knew she was trying to do too much; she knew I did not want to be consoled. She was demanding, while I was ungrateful. We relied on each other without giving much ground. We both wished Astrid were home with us. Both our jaws hardened when my father mentioned his girlfriend's name.

My mother saw Dr. Brady late after work on Thursdays. Sometimes I didn't see her until she picked me up at the Burger Hut, but as Christmas neared, I asked her to take me downtown to do my shopping while above the Hot Dog Shoppe she made sense of our new life. The streets were slushy and festooned with tinsel; in front of the Woolworth's a part-time Santa rang his bell tirelessly, badgering traffic. Butler had had a large blind school downtown years ago, and when the lights both ways went red and the white WALK sign came on, a steady ringing like a doorbell jimmied with a pin started so no one would get run over. I lingered by the black velvet–backed windows of Milo Williams jewelry, dreaming of what I'd give Lila. I could see myself kneeling on the sticky floor of the Penn, popping the box like an oyster. I had been working a lot this fall, and had more money in my account than ever before. I just did not know what to get everyone.

Two were easy. My father I would get tools. Exactly what kind would be discussed the next time he called; there was never any surprise involved. Astrid was into photography. I'd bought her film the last few Christmases. The rest was guesswork. I had some ideas for my mother—an electric blanket, a toaster oven—but they seemed dumb, not personal enough. My grandparents and aunt were always hard. And Lila.

I had my eye on a simple 24-karat chain in Milo Williams, and went so far as to ask the man behind the counter if I could see it. He slid the glass door aside and fished it out, gave it to me daintily, draping it over my hand. It was cold and a little stiff. I thought of the gold warm against Lila's neck. I pictured her squinting, happy with it.

"How much?" I asked, and the man told me.

I handed the chain back, draped it over his hand. If the date went wrong I'd be stuck with it. And if it went well, did I have to get something for Lily too?

Saturday afternoon my father told me not to worry. We were in the Nova, practicing three-point turns. I'd do one and drive fifty feet and do another and come back.

"This is her date," my father said. "Remember that, Arty. Be a gentleman and you'll both have a fine time. Do not be an octopus. Kiss her goodnight if she wants to be kissed.''

I did not want any advice beyond "Don't worry," and pointedly ignored the rest. We parallel-parked for a while, the rear hubcap scraping the curb.

"Okay," he said, signaling that we were done for the day, and I started to undo my belt.

"Whoa, whoa, whoa," he said. "How would you like to drive back to my place? Carefully."

"Yes," I said, trying not to blow it by being either too anxious or cool.

"I'll navigate," he said.

I had never driven on a highway before, and now I was getting on the interstate. The speedometer said I was doing 50. The Nova purred under my foot. I felt light, high.

"Check your mirrors," my father said. "Line up a point on the hood with the center line and keep it there. Feel how big the lane is."

"This is great," I said.

"Isn't it?" my father said. "You're doing great too."

He pointed to an exit just outside town and I steered into the chute.

"Gently brake," my father said. "Gently. Gently."

His new place was in a small L-shaped complex

with wooden siding stained by runoff from the gutters. MARYHAVEN, a carved sign at the entrance said. My father had his own numbered parking space. I stopped the car, put it in park and turned it off.

"Very nice," my father said, taking the keys. "Inside I have another surprise for you."

I thought it might be the stereo system I had been hoping for, or perhaps just the condition of the apartment itself, which, when he opened the door, pleased me. He had actual furniture, and plants, and a kitchen with a window. A dark-haired woman around my mother's age rose from a couch where she'd been reading. She had coffee in a mug I didn't recognize.

"Arthur, this is Marcia," my father said, "Marcia, my son Arthur."

"Arthur," she said, taking my hand. One of her front teeth was chipped. She was shorter than my mother and thinner and, unlike her, didn't wear any rings, no makeup either. The sweater she had on swallowed her.

"Nice to meet you," I said.

"Your father tells me you have a date tonight."

"That's right," I said, resentful.

"They're seeing the new *Godfather,*" my father put in.

"It's very good. Don and I both liked it, which is very rare."

She asked if I could stay for a cup of coffee but my father said I'd just come to see his new place. He showed me the bedroom and the bathroom, both full-sized. I remembered our old towels and the wicker peacock throne, but everything else was new to me, and exotic. By the bed he had an aquarium with angelfish, on Astrid's dresser a tape player bigger than Warren's. The empty cassette box was for Beethoven's Seventh Symphony.

"In A major," I said, astonishing them with Mr. Chervenick's trivia, "Opus 92."

"Yes," Marcia said, "your father says you're quite the musician." She was pretty and, I thought now, younger than my mother. Her jeans were white along the seams, the denim frayed.

"Not really," I said. "It's my first year."

"We'd better be heading back," my father said, "if we're going to get Cinderella here to the ball."

On the way out I tried to memorize the apartment, as if—a spy—I would decode its secrets when I got home.

"Come back," Marcia said at the door, still holding on to her coffee. "We'll have dinner."

"I will," I said.

In the car, before backing out, my father said, "I guess you were surprised, huh?"

"Yes," I said, "I was."

"Well, get ready for another, because we're thinking of getting married."

I had nothing to say to this.

"Not soon but eventually. Maybe sometime next year."

"Does Mom know about this?" I asked, as if she still held some authority.

"She doesn't like it but she knows about it."

"Does Astrid know?"

This stopped my father. "I don't know what your mother does and doesn't tell your sister."

"Mom didn't tell me," I said.

"I know. I wanted to tell you myself."

I looked out the windshield at the stained siding. Inside, lights were coming on. Every window was another apartment.

"Everything okay there, Arty?"

"Sure," I said. "I just don't want to be late."

When we returned to Foxwood, my mother seemed to know we'd seen Marcia. "We're going to be late," she scolded me, but her anger was intended for my father. While I got ready for my date with Lila, they argued in the living room. I didn't have time for a shower, which worried me. I did not want to hear what they said, and put on *Led Zeppelin III*, but even that was not loud enough, and all through "Gallows Pole" I heard my mother shouting, "I will not let you do this to me or to my son," and my father coming back with, "This is not about you and me anymore. I'm sorry, but that part of it is over."

I put on new underwear and my best corduroys, my white shirt with the top two buttons undone. I hauled on my cowboy boots, then thought better of the snow and settled for my everyday hiking boots. We would have to sit up front if we were late. From the living room came a crash.

"That's it," my father yelled. "Arty, I'm leaving."

I heard the door open and my mother outside, her voice tiny and stretched, screaming at him as he made for the Nova. I sat on the edge of my bed, calmly parting my hair. Like everything else that had happened that winter, I was not going to let this stop me from being happy.

T E N

GLENN'S RUNNING OUT OF GAS AND DOG FOOD. He's dodging the park police, leapfrogging the Boy Scout sleepover camps out at the lake. The cabins are painted shit brown and carved with initials, wire screens over the windows to keep raccoons from nesting in the mattresses. Two bunks jut from the wall. At first Glenn thought he should have brought more clothes; now he's glad he didn't. He's getting rid of things. He's even tossed the album with the pictures of Gibbsville. He carries a single wrinkled shot of Tara and Annie over his heart, sleeps with it in his hands.

He has his sleeping bag and a blanket borrowed from Rafe, but some nights it's so cold he has to risk starting the truck, and once it's warm, turns the heat up, leaning into the dash to feel the blast. Bomber lies in the footwell, cocking his head at the night owl radio.

"We should make that our confession," the syndicated preacher urges. "When God takes on our sickness, sin has no dominion over us—praise Jesus. When God takes on our disease, Satan has no hold on us. We know this because we've read in the Bible that there is no sin without Satan, that sin comes not from God but from the Adversary. God does not forget you; it is when you forget God, when you think God is slipping away from you, that the Adversary is slipping in. But listen to me now. God is still there with you now. He's never gone anywhere on you. He's right there with you now—all you've got to do this minute is accept Him back into your life."

Glenn lies across the seats, looking up at the perforated fabric of the ceiling, the dim bubble light, thinking that what the radio is saying is only partly true. No one is forgiven in advance. This man cannot take on his sin, cannot absolve him; that will only happen after the Rapture, when the dead are either taken up or cast down. It has nothing to do with a radio show or reading the Bible or the police. It has nothing to do with this fallen world.

He likes the next show better, a younger woman from North Carolina whose voice quivers and breaks like a country singer pleading with a lover, afraid she may be misunderstood. She sounds unsure, as if she's convincing herself. Glenn knows the feeling.

"You see, people don't want to live the life. It's boring, Rita, they say to me; it's no fun. But if you're born of the water then you know that loving God is never boring. 'And my faith shall slake your thirst like an overbrimming cup.' I think these people who are dried up and walking around dead are afraid. They don't know what that water's gonna do to them, and they're afraid."

The cab is warm. Glenn sees the gas gauge nodding toward EMPTY and turns everything off. Bomber grumps once, then settles in. He's still waiting to be fed. Glenn's sorry; there's only enough for tomorrow morning. He's hungry himself, his stomach hollow, nagging. Yesterday he had his last can of tuna fish for lunch, and for dinner the rest of the crackers. He ate them on the shore of the lake, watching the snow fall into the black water, thinking of Christmas in Gibbsville, the windows of his father's house frosted. He dipped the last cracker in the shallows, let it spread and melt soggily on his tongue, promised his father he would never forget him. He spent today in the cabin sketching what he remembered of him, warming his fingers over a candle. After a while he gave up; he saw he was drawing himself. He held the paper over the flame, watched it burn to black filmy ash on the floor.

Instead of eating he read the Psalms down by the water until it got dark.

> O Lord My God, in thee do I take refuge;
> Save me from all my pursuers, and deliver me,
> Lest like a lion they rend me,
> Dragging me away, with none to rescue.

He didn't think he'd be able to sleep tonight, and isn't surprised when he hears Bomber snoring. The woods are quiet, the wind still. His Bible is too underlined to read by candlelight. He wishes he could listen to the radio but he's afraid the battery might die. He thinks of North Carolina, the mist in the Blue Ridge Mountains heavy as smoke, the sea crashing in the dark off the Outer Banks. Born of the water, she said.

That's him. His name isn't even Marchand. He must have known his real name as a child, repeated it the way Tara did when, joking, he pretended not to remember hers: "Tara Elizabeth Marchand."

"Glenn Allen Marchand," he says, only his head poking out of the bag. Bomber snores on. The moon is caught in the steering wheel, the windshield pocked with stars. Jesus is his redeemer, his sword and staff. Jesus would never forget him.

He clutches the picture under his chin and closes his eyes. "Jesus," he says, "this is Glenn."

He wakes up at two-thirty, a quarter to four, a few minutes after six, then finally at nine, to Bomber licking him. Glenn holds the two white halves of Bomber's face, looks into his coughdrop-blue eyes. So close, his pupils remind Glenn of working on shock victims, of how he must have looked on the floor of his apartment, drowning in air. Now, just thinking about it, he feels himself floating out of his body, feels taken up. He remembers waking up on the floor, unaware that it was a tube down his throat choking him, that the hand smothering him held an oxygen mask. He hadn't been able to see straight. A white form glowed over him, and all he knew was that he was tired, that he was ready, even if he didn't believe, to go with this angel.

Bomber whines to get his attention back.

"Yes," Glenn says, "you're my big buddy," and scratches him between the ears.

He pours the sandy dregs of the bag into Bomber's dish, takes the other bowl to the shoreline for some water, then sits with the door open watching him eat. It's warmer this morning, his bootprints dark in the softening snow. The shallows steam; farther out, fog sits on the water. It's ten and threatening, a tinge of metal in the wind. He's in no rush; he's got all day. She'll be at her mother's after lunch. He steps out to check his wallet to make sure he's got enough for gas. Easy. When Bomber's finished, Glenn takes the dish and wings it like a Frisbee into the lake.

Bomber watches him pick up his water dish.

"What?" Glenn says. After he's thrown it, he takes a ten out, then pitches his wallet in. "Okay?" Glenn says, arms held wide. "Are we even?"

He polices the cabin, collects the crushed Ritz box, the cans, the beer bottles that aren't even his. "Give a hoot," Woodsy Owl warns from a bleached poster, "don't pollute." Around eleven he's ready to leave. On the way out of the campground he stops and tosses it all into a green, echoing trash barrel. He imagines calling Nan, what she'd say to him. He expected to hear from her after Tara died, but never did. He jumps a high curb, drives around the chained gate and exits the park, passing an empty ticket booth. He gets on the interstate and crosses a bridge over an arm of the lake, watches it go, glancing sideways until the trees intervene, then starts looking for cops.

The radio's on the same station as last night, playing neutered gospel music. It's too sweet for Glenn, all sopranos and syrupy strings. He finds his Cat Stevens eight-track and punches it in, right in the middle of "Moonshadow."

And if I ever lose my eyes, Cat sings, *I won't have to see no more.*

He stops for gas at a Sinclair along the strip in Prospect, holding the folded ten out between two fingers for the attendant, a skinny kid with a half-cast on his wrist. The kid squeegees the windshield, admiring Bomber, asks if Glenn wants him to check the oil. Glenn wonders what he'll think later, what he'll tell the police.

"Have a good weekend," the kid says.

"If I make it that far," Glenn says.

Rafe is at work. The windows are dark, icicles dripping from the eaves. Glenn leaves the blanket he borrowed on the porch glider, digs through the glovebox for a piece of paper to leave a note. He can't find one and rips an endpage out of his Bible.

"Thanks for the place to stay," he writes. "Take it easy. Your friend, Glenn-man."

It doesn't seem enough for everything Rafe has done for him, but he doesn't want to play it up or say the wrong thing. Coming back from the porch, he looks at his two sets of footprints in the snow and stops. He finds an untouched space to one side of the walk and falls backwards into the crust, waves his arms and legs to make an angel. He gets up and shakes the snow out of his coat, then squats and draws an arrow, with a finger writes "ME."

On the highway he tosses all his small stuff out the window, watching it scatter and bounce behind him in the mirror. His dirty shirts and pants, his balled socks. He puts his Bible on the dash beside his blue volunteer fire light and empties the rest of the glove compartment. Maps rattle in the wind, tear along their soft folds. He never hears the pennies ring.

"Quit staring at me," he tells Bomber.

He stops in the parking lot of a Foodland to stuff the sleeping bag into a Goodwill box. The bed of the pickup is littered with cans, but he doesn't have time to screw around with them. Where the carts are, he sees a collie chained to a post, waiting for its master. Bomber's watching the dog.

"It's up to you," Glenn says. "What do you want to do?"

On the way home he passes a state trooper going the other way. His heart clenches, throbs with shock.

He checks the speedometer, looks in the rearview mirror without turning his head. The cruiser gets smaller and smaller until finally its rack of lights dips below the road's horizon. "No problem," he says, speeding up, and the rush begins to leak off. He notices that he has a headache. He hasn't even gotten to the hard parts yet.

At home everything goes as planned. His father's car isn't in the driveway. Glenn gets out and clips Bomber to his chain. He doesn't want him to leave tracks in the house. The back door is unlocked and no one's home, though Glenn calls "Hello?" just to make sure. It's his mother's bridge day. Out of habit he peeks into the fridge. The idea of so much bright, cold food makes him sick and he lets the door swing shut. He goes to the gun cabinet in the back parlor where his father keeps his bird guns. Locked. The key should be in his mother's secretary, in the drawer with the curled strips of stamps, the obsolete denominations. It is.

Going back through the dining room, he stops to look at the hutch on which, along with his mother's mother's hand-painted Japanese dishes, stand pictures of himself in high school, Patty in her Navy blues, Richard and his kids in Tucson. On a shellacked slab of driftwood turned into a numberless clock, his mother and father wave from the seashore. Everyone seems happy. Her collection of souvenir baby spoons hangs in a special holder his father bought for her birthday. NIAGARA FALLS, the shields on the handles say, FORT LIGONIER, ATLANTIC CITY. Coming over, Glenn thought of going up to his room for a last look, but now, paralyzed by these mementos, understands that he can't and still go through with it.

He takes a new 12-gauge and a box of shells. More than he needs, he thinks. He relocks the glass door, returns the key. In the kitchen he rips a paper towel from the roll by the sink and, walking backward to the open door, wipes away his bootprints. On the back porch he thinks of leaving a note, but what would he say?

I'm sorry.

It didn't work.

Thank you.

It's not your fault.

With the shotgun broken over his arm, he unclips Bomber from his chain. Glenn opens the door for him and climbs in the other side. He slides the gun under his seat, fits the shells into the glovebox.

"Okay," he says to Bomber, "last chance to bail."

"All right," Glenn says, as if he's answered.

He keeps to the back roads, the unplowed county blacktops that cut the fields into squares. Cinders plink in the wheelwells. The richer poor live out here in trailers or rotting farmhouses shored up with plywood and silver panels of Celotex insulation. Smoke pours from their stovepipe chimneys. He passes a few newer cattle businesses; they're not farms, just long aluminum barns surrounded by cyclone fencing. The cattle are kept in pens, their necks clamped in feeding stanchions, growing fatter and fatter until a truck takes them away. It has begun to snow, the wind pushing it sideways across the road. In minutes he needs his wipers to see. The heater whirs. He sneaks along the back edge of the country club golf course, protected by the treeline, and thinks of her in her uniform. He meant to hit her, and then when she was on the ground, didn't.

It's not supposed to be easy, he thinks, and conjures Tara for support, that last day they spent together at the Aquazoo in Pittsburgh. The building was new, and humid inside. He had to carry their coats. A waterfall dropped from the lobby two stories to a pool glittering with pennies. Tara laughed at the penguins, chilly behind the glass. Shy, the octopus slept behind a rock. They wandered the lower level, bathed in the blue glow of the tanks, watching the light ripple over the dolphins' skin, holding hands. Glenn bought her an eraser shaped like a whale. Rafe was right; she was all he had. He thinks that he can do it, that he can go through with it. He's gone this far.

He turns the music off and they slow for the cemetery entrance. The snow is so new he can't be sure he's alone, but once they climb the rise Glenn sees he is. Cheap wreaths sit on wire stands, their ribbons fluttering. Toy flags flap. Bomber wants to come; Glenn lets him. He leaves the truck running, the heater and wipers going. Bomber dashes over the snow, looks back as if they might play a game.

Someone has been to visit in the last few days. Annie's father's vase holds a withered rose, red for love. Glenn takes it and places it at the base of Tara's stone. He kneels in the snow, bows his head over his folded hands. Several rows beyond, Bomber is turning circles. Behind him, the truck chugs.

"O Lord my God," Glenn recites, "if I have done this, if there is wrong in my hands, if I have requited my friend with evil or plundered the enemy without cause, let the enemy pursue me and overtake me, and let him trample my life to the ground, and lay my soul in the dust. Amen."

He picks his gloves up and stands there looking at her name, the last name false, not even his. That's how they'll bury him. It doesn't matter, he thinks; the trappings of this world are but clay. I am born of the water. On that last day I shall rise.

Glenn lies down on his back beside the grave and

waves his arms and legs. While he's making the angel, Bomber walks over and sniffs his face.

"Go," Glenn says, and he does.

As he's leaving, another truck pulls in, dark green, driven by an older man in a hunting cap. He doesn't return Glenn's wave.

To get to Annie's he has to either detour way around town or brave the interstate. The lunch rush is over, but he doesn't want to risk stopping at every red light. He swings onto an entrance ramp, turns the music up to adjust for the noise. *Oooh baby baby it's a wild world,* Cat sings. *It's hard to get by just upon a smile.* The song's right, Glenn thinks; he doesn't see a single policeman.

He takes the high school exit, cruises past the full parking lot. They made love there for the first time. In the summer in his Impala. He remembers the line of sweat under her bra, how cold it was out of their clothes, how his knees squeaked on the upholstery. Below them, the city shimmered like a dying campfire. Late June, the promise of summer. He felt something give inside her, and she grunted through clenched teeth, her eyes bright with pain. She hadn't told him she was a virgin; he thought he had hurt her. "I'm okay," she kept saying, trying to console him. The next day the backseat reeked of blood and he drove

253

with the windows open. He bought two dangling pine trees. Sherwood Forest, Annie called them. Sure would. She used to thrash her head around, chew her lower lip, laugh. The building hasn't changed, or the view, only the cars and the kids in them. It's a mystery, Glenn thinks, that he's on the wrong end of.

No one's poking out of the middle school road. He's paranoid, expecting police everywhere. He's ready to glide by Turkey Hill without stopping if there are any cars around the house. The snow has slacked off but is still falling, fat sugary flakes that dissolve before the wipers hit them. The trees are starting to turn white. He slows before the road, gets a good look at Clare Hardesty's, her empty driveway, then continues through the intersection, not stopping.

"What do you see?" he asks Bomber, who, having recognized where they are, is whimpering and pawing at the door.

Glenn glances sideways, picking up the blue of the water tower, then back to the road, to the side, the road. He doesn't see anyone. The fields are bare, the Maverick gone. As far as he can tell, the house is dark. Two-oh-five. It's gratifying. He's worked hard for this.

He turns at the first road and does a three-pointer, comes back the other way. He slows, signals and makes the left onto Turkey Hill.

Now I've been smiling lately, Cat Stevens sings, *think-*

ing about the good things to come. Glenn punches it out, clicks it off. Driving along the edge of the woods, he peers back through the trees, looks over his shoulder at the road. Nothing, nobody.

"You're going to stay in the truck," he explains to Bomber.

He passes the drive and the mailbox. The flag's down. He was right, the house is dark. In the turn-around he has to get out to move a trash barrel blocking the road, then when he's past, has to move it back. Bomber's interested, and both times steals Glenn's seat. "Scoot over," Glenn says. He wonders how long it will take for the snow to cover his tracks.

He parks where the road dead-ends at a snowy mound. Hunching over to get the shotgun from under the seat, he inadvertently hits the horn.

He pops his head up, breathing hard.

The woods are still, the snow dropping plumb.

"Watch what you're doing."

He pulls the gun out and thumbs in a pair of shells. He splits the rest of the box between his pockets.

"I don't want you barking," he warns Bomber, and before leaving him, rubs the plush ridge of fur on his chest. "I'll be back."

Outside it's surprisingly warm—and quiet, only birds and melt-off dripping, the thrum of distant traffic. The snow is snowball snow and the footing's good.

He can smell the mud underneath. He picks his way through the brush, one hand clutching the stock of the gun, the other out for balance, fingertips braced against tree trunks. As he nears the pond trail, he can hear the spillway. It reminds him of the search, how he was stumbling through the pines when the bullhorn called them all in, his father's intuition off by miles.

The trooper with him had a walkie-talkie, and checked in. "I'm with the husband," he said, and let the button up.

"Tell him," a fuzzy voice squelched, "that we're very sorry."

The trooper ran with him to the creek where they said they'd seen her. Annie was there, in her mother's arms, crushing a Kleenex to her face, angrily keening. Brock stood off to one side, afraid to touch her.

"Where is she?" Glenn asked the inspector.

"The boys say they saw your daughter here, moving with the current." He pointed to the drainpipe running under the hillside.

Glenn jumped into the water. It wasn't three feet high. The trooper wrestled him out, held him away from it as if breaking up a fight. His thighs were freezing, his jeans heavy. Even now he thinks they should have let him go. The police had to call in a diver. By the time he was ready it was dark and they had to stand there in the glare of utility lights hung from bushes, waiting for the wet-suited man to pull her out by the ankles. Again, Glenn jumped into the water, soaking a borrowed pair of pants. Annie screamed and screamed.

He hasn't been back in these woods since then. He forgets how much they used to love sitting in the back-yard on summer nights with a beer, listening to the crickets, in August watching for meteor showers. Annie had wanted a garden, and rabbits for Tara. Glenn promised to build her a clubhouse. That's all gone, he thinks. It's dumb to bring it up now.

But creeping up on the house, he can't help seeing that the gutters are clogged with leaves, that the lawn furniture on the screenporch is rusting. There must be a year's worth of Fresca bottles. He'd had hopes for this house, plans. When did everything turn to shit?

The door to the screenporch is locked. He takes his keys and pokes a hole in the screen, rips it and reaches in, scratching his wrist. A little blood. It heartens him. He leans the shotgun against the back door and checks the bathroom window. He pulls the arm of his jacket over his fist and punches the pane above the lock. It tinkles and falls to the carpet. Somewhere a dog barks—not Bomber. Glenn opens the window and pulls back the curtain, breaks the gun and scissors through. The glass snaps under his boots on the bathmat. He closes the window and draws the curtain again.

He goes through the house as if it's on fire, room by room, the way they taught him in rescue. He sits on Annie's bed and rifles the nightstand. Her father's revolver is gone.

"You're not dumb," he admits.

He looks in her top dresser drawer to be sure, stirring her belts and watch straps and pantyhose packages. In the closet sits a shopping bag of gift-wrapped Christmas presents. For who, he wonders. She's written the initials small on the tape so she'll remember: MVD, DVD, RVD. Nothing for Tara, nothing for him.

"Merry Christmas," he says, and kicks the bag back into the closet.

Tara's room is newly vacuumed, the bed made, the bunny he gave her waiting with open arms. A naked Barbie lies in a nest of clothes on Tara's tiny vanity. Glenn kneels and looks into the oval mirror and is surprised to see the barrel of the shotgun in his hand, the thin coating of oil smudged with his fingerprints. His father used to scold him for holding it wrong. He'd take the gun from him and say Glenn could have it back when he learned to treat his weapon with respect. When they came in from the fields, his father lectured Glenn as he cleaned the guns with a soft cloth at the dinner table. He let Glenn set them back in the cabinet. His mother consoled him with hot chocolate. "Your father wants you to be responsible," she said.

He looks out Tara's window onto the backyard. His footprints seem to be in a hurry, on a beeline from the woods to the porch door. It's not even two-thirty; by five his tiretracks will be filled in. She's going to be surprised.

Downstairs he checks the front windows. From the chair beside the door he can see up the road past the streetlamp. When he leans back he's invisible. He rests the gun across his lap, folds his arms. He looks at the room as if it's a doctor's office, noting everything. Annie's tennis shoes sit by the front door, waiting for better weather. On the coffee table sprawls a glossy food magazine, open to a lush shot of some chocolate dessert. His stomach hurts and he clears his throat to make it go away. In the dead TV screen his head is just a speck above the curved couch. He waves to see it better. There he is, today's special guest.

After twenty minutes he leans the gun against the back of the couch and takes off his jacket. He stretches, rolls his head on his neck, yawns. He didn't sleep well last night. He doesn't remember dreaming anything. Since yesterday he's been bothered by the psalm, the image of a lion standing with his front paws on his chest, shredding Glenn like newspaper.

He drops to the carpet and bows head over hands. "O let the evil of the wicked come to an end, but establish Thou the righteous, Thou who triest our minds and hearts, Thou righteous God." He stays there with his eyes closed. "My name is not Glenn," he says. "I am born of the water. I am one with the spirit of Jesus, who will never let me die. I will not be fooled by this world of shades, but will live in heaven everlasting. Amen."

He stands, strong, ready to do this now. Any doubt, any weakness, has left him, and faith fills that emptiness. He is the light and the way. The woman from last night was right, he thinks; loving Jesus is never boring.

In the refrigerator he finds some lunchmeat. Olive loaf and chipped ham. He doesn't bother with bread, just rolls the meat into tubes and pops them in his mouth. He stands, holding the door open, digging through the drawer for some cheese, when his throat closes and heaves. He lunges across the drainboard and, sick, braces himself against the counter, his retching echoed and amplified by the sink. After the first jerk he has nothing to throw up, only bitter yellow strings. The effort makes him gasp, raises tears. He runs the tap, swishes a mouthful and spits. When he straightens up, he finds his headache is back.

He goes to the front window, afraid someone may be coming. The road's empty. The snow falls. It's barely past three and he wants to sleep. He sits in his chair and hauls the shotgun onto his lap again, turns toward the road. The afternoon is beginning to fade, the light in the room gray, shadows deepening in the corners. Glenn thinks of her at her mother's, sitting at the kitchen table, making excuses for losing Tara, for screwing Brock. When he was working at the scrapyard, he used to think of them doing it in the bed he'd paid for and he'd have to drive out in his ridiculous cart to the back fence and smash something. He liked that job. She took that from him too.

He paces, he sits at the kitchen table. He tromps upstairs and kneels by Tara's bed, brings the bunny back downstairs with him and props it on the couch. She'll be home soon, coming in the front door. He'll have to get her purse away from her, find the gun. The rest he has planned. He needs to be strong, to believe.

Back in his chair he nods off, wakes with a shock as if stabbed in a nightmare. Four forty-five. The room is dark; outside, the streetlamp is on, the sky a shade lighter than the pines. He thinks of Bomber and hopes he's asleep. He puts his coat on and pumps the gun, turns to the window and waits.

He'll know when it's her. The Maverick has orange turn signals on the grille, inboard of the head-lights.

The snow drops through the streetlamp. The furnace clicks on, ignites with a whoosh. The sun is down now; Glenn is amazed how much light there still is. The wall along the staircase is striped with the shadow of the banister. He's marveling at it when he hears a car and turns to see the two dots of its lights in the window.

It's too far to see the turn signals, but when it glides beneath the streetlamp, the color gives it away. It's her.

He slides out of the chair, crouching, keeping an eye on the lights. As they near the drive he scuttles over to the door and stands, the gun held across his chest. He can feel the weakness descend on him again, and he remembers Elder Francis's teaching. His mercy is of this world, and worthless. His flesh is grass.

O let the evil of the wicked come to an end.

The car door thunks. He's got to get her purse. He presses his back against the wall beside the light switch.

But establish Thou the righteous.

Footsteps on the porch, then jingling, the crunch of the key in the lock. The bolt turns with a click; the door opens, swinging toward him.

She reaches for the light switch and he grabs her arm, spins her inside before she has time to react, scream, anything. Her purse falls to the floor between them. She sees the gun and tries to back away, but he has a good grip on her wrist.

"Glenn," she says, "oh my god, oh my god, Glenn."

He's too close to point the gun at her. He pushes her backwards onto the couch and scoops up her purse. She's crying. He breaks the gun over his arm and retreats to the corner by the door, bumping it shut.

"Please," she says, and stands, her hands out in front of her. "I didn't do anything. Glenn."

"Calm down." He can't get the thing open; she's begging him. "Please," he says, "just be quiet."

The clasp gives way and everything pours out at his feet. The revolver bounces on the carpet. It's bigger than he remembers, a cheap knockoff of a Colt. He watches her as he kneels to pick it up. It's loaded, heavy in his palm.

"It's your father's," he says, half asking. "I remember it from the other night."

Annie shakes her head as if this isn't happening. "Glenn," she pleads.

"Shhh," he says. "Quiet."

He rounds the couch, the revolver at his side, pointed toward the floor. He gets behind her, and she turns to watch him.

"Turn around," he says. "Don't worry about what I'm doing."

He leans the shotgun next to the TV.

"Turn the lights on," he says, but she doesn't budge. "I don't want to be angry with you now. Especially now. So turn them on. You can move, it's all right."

She keeps him in sight as she backs around the couch. He doesn't even have the gun on her. When she flips the switch, the windows blink with a colored light. He bends down to see in the front yard the small dogwood strung with bulbs.

"Now lower the blinds."

She does.

"Thank you," Glenn says. He sits down on the couch. She's stopped crying, interested in what he's up to, looking for a way out. "Are you supposed to work tonight?" he asks, though he knows she's due in at six.

"Yes."

"Did you eat yet?"

"No."

"Do you want something?"

"Please don't do this."

"Shhh," he says.

"Please, Glenn, just let me go. I'll leave here, I'll go somewhere, I swear—"

"Don't talk. It'll only make it worse for both of us. I don't want to do this either."

"Then don't."

"No," he says. "We're going to do this. We're going to do it and that'll be it. I'm tired of this crap and I want it over." He sees that he's waving the gun around to make his point; she's mesmerized by it. He lays it beside his thigh where she can't see it. "Sit down," he says, gesturing to the chair by the window. "Sit."

"What do I have to do?" she says.

"Shhh. Take your boots off."

"No."

"Please. Take your boots off." He stands and lets her see the gun, and she starts unlacing them. "And your socks. Leave your coat on. You can undo it, but keep it on. All right, let's go into the kitchen. That's it. Turn the hall light on. Good. And the switch to the right here. Very good. And have a seat at the table. Turn the chair sideways so your legs aren't under it."

With his free hand he opens the cupboard by the oven and, making a racket, pulls a large pot out. He turns on the hot tap, lets the water warm, then fills the pot. Still holding the gun, he places the pot on the floor by her feet. He lays the gun gently on the linoleum and dips both hands into the water, presses them to her cold feet.

"Oh god oh god oh god," she heaves. "Glenn, please, Glenn."

He rubs the water over her bones, over the meaty sole, the toes. He cups a handful and rinses her feet clean.

As he's finishing, she kicks him in the chest, but not hard enough to move him. He holds her legs while she curses him, screaming and flailing at his head. One or two blows make him flinch, but she's not strong enough, not big enough. He's been ready to do this a long time. He pushes her off, holds her by the throat, but she won't stop. He covers her eyes with his other hand, presses her against the chairback so she chokes. She can't see the gun, can't reach it, and finally she tires, reverts to crying. When she's done, he fetches a dish towel and dries her feet.

"I'm sorry," he says. "I am. Don't you know I love you?"

She doesn't say anything to this. She's hanging her head, no longer looking at him. Her neck is red where his hand was. The gun doesn't interest her anymore.

"You don't have to believe me," he says.

"Fuck you," she says.

"Let's go."

She won't stand and he has to pull her up by one arm. He pushes her ahead of him toward the back door, but she falls down. He sticks the gun in the back of his belt and lifts her, walks her to the door as if she's drunk. He clicks the spotlight on and the back- yard shines, the snow twinkling, shadowed blue. His footprints from this afternoon are gone.

The snow makes him blink, flakes tickling his ears. Wind, traffic. Before they reach the woods, she's be- gun to mumble from fright.

"It's all right," he says, rubbing her shoulders. "It won't be long. Everything's going to be all right."

Her feet sink into the snow. He wishes it could be any other way, and, unsure of himself, picks her up, keeping her arms where he can see them. She's weep- ing, curling herself around him for comfort. He hopes she's quit. This is the hardest part.

He sticks the gun in his coat pocket and, with her on his lap, slides down the hill on his bottom. In the darkness, water rushes over the spillway. The constant sound helps him. He holds the back of her jacket and steers her along the shore. From far off comes music, a fragment of some march everyone knows, all drums and trumpets. Above, a truck passes on the interstate, erasing it. She stumbles ahead of him.

"No," she repeats, twisting the word, "no, no, no, no, no."

"It's all right," he says, "it's not long now."

They cross the bridge over the spillway and follow a slippery trail along the creek. It's overgrown; they shoulder snow from the bushes. Branches whip their arms. He checks his coat for the gun, closes his hand around the grip. He doesn't want anything long and drawn out, just to get it done. He doesn't know how to do this.

The creek stops at the pipe going into the hillside. The water's high, gurgling tinnily. She stops. He stops.

"Kneel down," he says.

She understands, and kneels facing the water, the soles of her feet sticking out behind. He takes the gun from his pocket. He touches her hair, what he loved about her first, bends her head forward.

"Tell me when you're ready," he says.

"I'm ready," she replies.

"I'm sorry," he says, but waits, half turns to hear the music.

"I'm ready," she says again.

The gun bucks and she splashes. Birds frightened by the shot flap above him, invisible in the dark. She's floating, only a hand clenching and unclenching, trying to grip the water. Glenn empties the gun at her, stands a second staring at the holes in her coat, the whiteness of her feet, then runs.

Crossing the spillway, he notices he still has the gun, and drops it in the water. He falls on the hill, claws his way to the top, where he sees the lights of the house through the trees. The snow is heavy but running is effortless. The music's gone. He can't hear a thing, only this wildness inside. It's done, he thinks. He did it.

He throws the porch door open, the back door. He runs down the hall, through the kitchen and into the living room. The shotgun's where he left it. Forgetting his plan, he rushes out the front door and across the yard. The water tower dwarfs him.

Bomber barks until Glenn tells him to quit. The windows are frosted over. Glenn gets in, tossing the shotgun onto the passenger seat. The truck turns over on the first try but the wipers won't go. Keeping the lights off, he searches under the seat for a scraper, but like everything else, he's thrown it away. Somewhere he's lost his gloves, and he has to attack the snow with his bare hands. He does the front window and his side, gets in again. He opens his window and sticks his head out to back up the road, and then forgets the trash barrel, rams the bumper into it.

"Fuck."

The wheels don't grab at first; he fishtails past the

mailbox, the engine roaring. He knows he's panicking and squeezes the steering wheel to regain control over himself.

"Lights," he says, and flips them on.

As he nears the stop sign, he sees the Hardestys are home, the curtain drawn across the living room window. Waiting for a car to pass, he breaks the shotgun and tucks it under his seat.

"Okay, take it easy."

He looks at Bomber but has nothing to say to him.

Passing the middle school, he hears sirens, probably on the interstate. He's right, he can see the red sweep of the lights coming on the other side of the bridge's hump.

"Shit."

Two, maybe three. He's fucked, probably by Clare Hardesty—or his parents, he thinks. His original plan was to make it back to the lake, but that's not going to happen. He swings into the high school lot, thinking it's not a bad substitute. Butler for the lake, his false home for his real one. Born of the water, not this world of clay.

It's past six, but a few cars are just leaving. He sees a tall boy lugging a tuba, another with a snare drum under his arm. It's the band he heard. A group of them cross the lot in his headlights. Behind him on Far Line a state trooper shoots by, siren whining. Glenn's not paranoid; he can hear more in the distance. They'll want his ass bad but he won't let them. He never planned on surviving this.

He cruises past the front doors, where a few kids are waiting to be picked up. Bomber watches them, wagging his tail. He's been cooped up too long, probably has to pee. Glenn follows along the building to the end, then turns the corner. The back part of the lot is empty and well lit, the dumpsters snow-covered. They used to throw stones at the vapor lamps so they could make out here. He remembers the exact parking spot, the third from the end. He pulls into it and kills the lights, keeps the heater going.

"Do you have to go out?" he asks Bomber, who mobs him.

"Okay, okay," he says.

Before opening the door, Glenn holds him, nuzzles his bristly head, breathes the doggy odor of his coat. The fucking bunny, he's forgotten it again. The thought of it on the couch is enough to make him break down.

Bomber doesn't understand, and licks his tears.

"You're my buddy," Glenn says, and hugs him again, feeling his ribs give. He opens the door for him. Bomber leaps and twists in the snow, only partly showing off. Glenn thinks he's beautiful; he could never be happy like that.

It's coming down too heavily to see town, only a muffled light in the clouds. Glenn turns off the heater, turns off the engine. Bomber's over by the picnic tables, sniffing. Maybe he's strange, Glenn thinks, but he doesn't want Bomber to see him the way he had to see Tara. He makes sure his door's unlocked so they won't have to break in, lays his keys on his Bible, open to the Seventh Psalm. If there is evil in these hands . . . He reaches under the seat for the gun, and the horn honks.

"You are such a fuck-up," Glenn says.

E L E V E N

AT THE END OF OUR DATE I kissed Lila Raybern good-night. She kissed me back harder than I expected and took her glasses off so they wouldn't poke me in the eye. We stood on the landing in the cold. My mother had gone inside to give us some privacy, though I was sure she was spying from the front window. Lila had been eating wintergreen Life Savers, and the clean heat of her mouth thrilled me. I said I would see her tomorrow and watched her walk across the snow to her building. She waved before going in. In bed I said her name to the darkness. I decided I would buy the chain.

From band practice I went straight to the Burger Hut. After eight, when it was slow, I called Lila from the kitchen. I helped Mr. Philbin close and he gave me a ride home. More often than not my mother was asleep. I let myself in, wolfed some Pop-Tarts and watched TV before turning in, thinking of how I'd see Lila in the morning. We sat together on the bus now, effortlessly betraying Warren and Lily.

At school everyone talked about Annie and how weird it was. The afternoon—the evening—of the killing, I didn't remember seeing Glenn pass through in his pickup. I had to read about it the next day in the *Eagle,* and when I did I realized that for a few minutes we had been—besides the janitor, who was credited with finding him—the only two people there. My mother was late picking me up. I stood in the light from the lobby, watching the snow, wondering where all the sirens were going, where the dog that wouldn't stop barking was.

I told no one this, not even Lila. When asked, I admitted only that Annie babysat me a few times. Our families weren't that close, I said. At home, my mother would not discuss it, and when it was mentioned on the news, she changed the channel. The memorial service was private; we were not invited. My mother sent Mrs. Van Dorn a card, which she signed for both of us, and speculated out loud whether my father would remember to.

I still had not had dinner with my father and Marcia. We were supposed to the Saturday after our last home game. It was a secret. My mother had forbidden me to see or even speak to Marcia, but this did not stop my father. Every time he took me out to slide around the snowy parking lot in his Nova, there she was at his apartment, reading and listening serenely to Brahms, with hot chocolate ready for us. My father kissed her at the door, which did not shock me, but which did not seem like him either. I could not get used to her tooth, or the way they smiled at each other, as if waging a silent conversation. When he sat beside her on the couch, his hand found hers, his thumb stroking the back of her fingers. His attentions reminded me of Lila and how we touched, but unpleasantly. I wondered aloud how Tony Dorsett and Pitt were doing; he said he'd have to buy a set just so I could watch it—as if he had no interest in the game, which was untrue. At home all Saturday and Sunday afternoon, he wallowed on the couch downstairs, soaking in a six of Iron City along with the entire college and pro lineups. And when did he begin listening to classical music? It was all for her, I thought, the way I decided to stop getting high so much after Lila said she didn't like it. I wished that, like Warren jagging me, I could give my father shit about his sudden changes, but I knew that, like me, he wouldn't appreciate it, no matter how true.

My mother let slip—over dinner or in the car, watching TV or getting ready for work—that my father was confused, sometimes implying that he was mentally ill and needed treatment. I did not tell her that he seemed happy to me. I was careful never to mention Marcia in the house, but every so often my mother would come out with: "She'll never marry him. I know women like that, and she will never marry him."

Once when she came back wobbly from a night on the town, she said, "That woman of your father's is no good. There's a name for women like her."

It was a Friday and Lila was with me, watching "Chiller Theatre." Neither of us said anything. My mother's shoes dangled from one hand; her lipstick was smudged, her hair rumpled as if she'd been in a fight. She dropped onto the couch beside us and lit up.

"Your father doesn't even see it. He doesn't want

to see it." She leaned across me and spoke to Lila as if giving her advice. "He left me for her, did you know that? That was the biggest mistake he'll ever make, mark my words. What is this movie?"

In minutes she was asleep beside me, her shoes nestled in her lap. Lila said she'd better go, and though the movie wasn't half over, I didn't argue. I walked her to the door. My mother was snoring, sprawled now across the empty couch.

"Is she all right?" Lila asked on the landing after I kissed her goodnight.

"She will be," I said.

But she was not, and as Christmas neared she began to talk more often about her unhappiness, which I did not need to hear. She said she prayed to God I would not turn out like my father. She said everybody knew what kind of woman she was and what kind of woman Marcia Dolan was. She said if she did not have to take care of me she would leave this town and never show her face here again, didn't I know that? When she didn't talk to me, I could be happy. I had Lila and I didn't need anything or anyone else. I listened to my mother with the same skepticism I had earlier reserved for my father, and when she had left the room, gave the finger to her long-departed back.

"What are you doing?" Astrid said over the

phone. My mother had begun calling her every few days, regardless of the hour. "Haven't you listened to anything I've said?"

"What do you want me to do?"

"Stop thinking about yourself, for one thing."

I said nothing. She was right, but wrong in making it sound like my fault.

"Do you want me to come home?" she asked. "Is that what you want?"

In the transatlantic silence I thought of my mother, my father and Marcia, Annie and her little girl. Every session Dr. Brady made me talk about her. I still hadn't dreamed of her, but several times a day I saw her floating in her muddied snowsuit and had to shake my head to get rid of her. Sometimes I pictured her while I waited to be picked up, scarfing down my two chili dogs. The drainpipe and the ice. The mitten slowly nosing the surface. The snow. I'd finish and feel the onions searing my throat and sometimes the heat made my eyes water. I went outside, where it was dusk and people were doing last-minute shopping. In the car I didn't tell my mother how I felt. I hadn't told Astrid, though I hoped she knew.

"Yes," I said.

"Well I can't," Astrid said. "You're just going to have to deal with it yourself. There's nothing I can do right now anyway."

Then what, I wanted to ask, was *I* supposed to do?

I could make breakfast. The next day I got up early and put the coffee on and made fried eggs and toast for myself and ate them, all the time waiting for my mother to smell everything and come see what I had done. When I had finished, her door was still closed. I poured her coffee and splashed in just enough milk, set it at her place and called for her. It was seven-twenty; she should have been showered and dressed by now. I knocked on her door and then pushed it open.

The shades were down, the red numbers of her clock sharp in the darkness. She was in bed but not asleep, propped up on her pillows. Her arms lay limp on the spread, a Kleenex clutched in one hand. On the floor by her night table sat a scattering of used tissues. She sniffed and looked at me helplessly, and I tried not to be angry.

"I'm not going in today," she said. "I don't feel well."

"I made coffee."

"That was sweet."

"Do you want me to bring it in?"

"That would be nice."

I went into the kitchen and brought her coffee back and put it on her night table. She smiled but didn't touch it.

"You don't mind if I stay home today," she asked.

"No," I said.

"Arthur," she said, but said nothing more for a while. I stood there in the dim room. The coffee steamed. The minute turned on the clock.

"I'm just very tired," she explained. "Do you understand?"

"Yes," I said.

"I'll be all right, I'm just worn out right now."

I didn't know what to say to this.

"I've got to get my bus," I said.

"I know. You go ahead. Don't worry about me."

"You don't have to pick me up. I've got practice and then work."

"So you'll be home late." It seemed more than a disappointment to her. An accusation.

"The regular time," I said.

She turned away, uninterested. "Go. You'll be late."

Outside, it was still dark. Lily was sick again. Lila asked why I was pissed off so early in the morning.

"Why do you think?" I asked, and then apologized.

"It's all right," she said, and I thought, as we walked up toward the bus stop, that this was another part of my life that my parents were creeping into and ruining. I felt wrong for abandoning my mother, leaving her with the lights out and the shades down, but it was not my fault. Didn't Dr. Brady tell me to always remember that?

When I came in that night, my mother was asleep. She'd left the light in the kitchen on. The house was cold. Her coffee mug was in the sink, along with one other dish and a soup spoon. Ice cream, maybe, or cereal. I wondered if she'd left the house all day. I wondered how long this would go on.

The next morning she was up before me, but in her robe. Eating my eggs, I watched the clock over the sink. She sat across from me, smoking and nursing her coffee. Please get dressed, I thought, please. She caught me looking at her and then the clock and sighed.

I took a bite of toast and buried my eyes in my plate.

"I need time, Arthur. Will you give me some time?"

"Sure," I said.

"Thank you."

She took her mug to the sink. I kept eating. I was surprised how easily I had given up on her. Now that it was done, I was glad not to discuss it. I had endured the moment; I had won. Yet that night, faced with my reflection in the Fry-o-lator, as I tried not to picture the pipe sucking the mitten in, I saw my mother running water over the tip of her cigarette and then tossing the wet butt in the garbage.

Thursday she saw Dr. Brady while I priced gold chains at Milo Williams and browsed through the True Value for a tool my father might need. The lightpoles were festooned with huge tinsel bells and candles. We didn't even have a tree, and the colored lights running marquee-like around Woolworth's windows annoyed me. I got back to the Hot Dog Shoppe on time, afraid of making her wait, but she hadn't come down yet. The air was heavy with grease. I wasn't hungry and ordered a cherry Slurpee, and then a lemon-lime when she hadn't showed. I was almost done with it when she pushed through the door. She had her driving gloves on. In one hand she clutched a tissue. It would never stop, I thought.

"I think that's what I needed," she said in the car, but didn't explain. Inexplicably, I felt jealous of Dr. Brady. But the next day she went to work, and silently I thanked him.

Saturday was our last home game and our final try at the tornado. Driving over, my mother wondered if I wanted her to stay and watch. She had never come to any of our games before and she was dressed to go shopping.

"No," I said, "that's all right."

"I will if you want me to," she said.

"No," I said.

She should have stayed, because we actually did the tornado right. We stood sweating on our assigned spots as the crowd rose, then hustled off double-time. Mr. Chervenick pounded us on our backs as we filed into the runway. He leaped between the rows, waving his score. "Tremendous!" he crowed. "You are the ones!" We marched—still with precision, though the show was over—through the parking lot and inside to the gym to change. Our shouts reached down the long, empty halls. When we had come out of our respective locker rooms and gathered wet-haired on the basketball court, Mr. Chervenick addressed us from the bleachers.

"I am very proud of you. You have all come a very long way since this summer, and I feel lucky to have had the opportunity to work with you. This is a year I will always remember. I hope you will too."

"Yeah yeah yeah," Warren said beside me.

"Don't be a jerk," I said.

"What's with you?" he asked after we had given ourselves three cheers. And what could I say—that I liked Mr. Chervenick, that I wished everyone were more like him, even if he was full of shit?

"Nothing," I said, and being friends, we let it drop.

My mother pulled up with a Sears bag in the backseat. I told her about the tornado. She was impressed for a second, then asked what my father and I had planned for the rest of the afternoon.

"I don't know," I lied.

"What time is he coming to pick you up?"

"Around four?" I said, though we had agreed on it. I even knew what we were going to eat—homemade pizza.

At home I waited in the living room with the Pitt game on softly. My father was late, which once would have been unusual. He no longer came to the door but just honked. I listened for the chug of his Nova over the play-by-play. By the end of the first quarter it wasn't close anymore. Tony Dorsett sliced through the Navy secondary, running up his numbers. At halftime my mother closed the door to her room to wrap whatever she'd bought, and I went to the front window. The sun was orange in the trees, shadows stretching across the snow toward our building. The sky was bright high up but fading gray down low. It was the time of day my father would break out the potato chips and dip and the card he bought for a dollar at work and see how his picks were doing. Now, as he had when we were living in our old house, ABC's Jim Lampley went through the top twenty. I looked in the fridge, going shelf to shelf before getting myself a Pepsi and sitting back down.

"Do you want me to call him?" my mother said. "It's almost five-thirty."

"I know," I said.

"I can call him. I don't mind. He should at least be fulfilling his responsibilities to you."

"Sure," I said. "Call him."

I turned back to the set and pretended not to listen to her dial. Pitt had the second string in.

My mother clacked the receiver down.

"No answer."

I turned to look at her. She picked up and tried again.

"Nothing," she shrugged. "This is just like him. I'm sorry, Arthur, I don't know what's wrong with your father anymore."

"It's all right," I said, which was dumb.

"It's not all right with me, and it shouldn't be all right with you." She started to go on about it, following me down the hall to my room. She stopped in the door. I turned on my stereo, lay down on my bed and put my headphones on. The Who, *Quadrophenia*, Side 4. The needle traced the record's shiny edge, the hiss growing into the boom and hush of the ocean. I closed my eyes, and when I opened them, my mother had closed the door.

She tried him again after dinner. I don't even remember what we had. I heard her dialing and concentrated on the TV. Two firemen in a kitchen saying something—a joke about chili. My mother wasn't saying anything. Four-alarm chili. The laughtrack laughed.

"Not there," she said, and I was angry with her for calling at all. I waited until she had gone to bed to stand outside on the landing and get stoned. I turned my light off and put my headphones on, Side 1 this time.

Sunday she reached him in the middle of the Steeler game. She announced that she was going to see if he'd returned from wherever he'd been. I pretended I wasn't interested. Unwinding, the dial clicked.

"Well," my mother said loudly in the kitchen. "We were looking for you yesterday."

His explanation was not long.

"Will you be able to make it next Saturday? Seeing that it *is* the last weekend before Christmas."

"That's good, because your son would like to see you." She took a deep, satisfying drag of her cigarette, and as she waited for his reply, I thought I saw her smile. She liked this.

"I don't want to hear about your problems, Don. I've got enough of my own. I could have told you that —I tried to tell you that. Don't tell me I didn't try. You've made your bed, mister, and whoever does or doesn't sleep in it is none of my concern. Don't you dare use her as an excuse for not seeing Arthur, don't you dare."

She was sitting on a stool by the counter, but now she crushed out her butt in the sink and got up to pace.

"Bullshit," she said, and laughed. "Do you know what I say? I say good for her. She's not such a little idiot after all."

"No," she said. "Don, no. No. That is bullshit and you know it. You are not going to turn this around onto me. There is no way."

She halted suddenly and put up one hand as if to stop him from talking. "Ha!" she said.

I quietly moved to my room. I could hear her through the door. Not every word, but enough. I lay down on my bed and looked at my stereo, then at the ice flowers on the bottom of my window. They ran in zigzags like stitches, spiked like barbed wire. Outside, high in the sky, a single ball of a cloud drifted through the blue, dwindling sunward like a runaway balloon. I imagined how Foxwood looked from up there—the miniature buildings and cars and trees— and how the drive up to the bus stop met the county road that cut through snowed-over fields and across smaller blacktops linking farms and trailer parks and auto graveyards until it hit the outskirts of Butler where I used to live. I wondered about our old house, and my old room. Who was in it, and did they feel me there sometimes? I didn't think so, but in my mind I walked the hallway to the kitchen and down the stairs to the basement, where my father would be watching the game I had just left, and so slowly, savoring every detail on my way, that I no longer heard my mother in the other room.

"That was your father," she said when she came in. She was surprised to see me without my headphones. "He apologized for yesterday. He said he'd like to reschedule for next weekend, and I told him it was all right with me if it's all right with you. Is it?"

"Sure," I said.

"You know that all of this has nothing to do with you. Don't be too angry with him. He's having some problems of his own right now." She said this with concern, as if she was worried about him. I did not understand why—if she was glad that Marcia had left him, which she was—and decided she was lying about how she felt. She was doing it for my sake when there was no need. Right then, I did not want her to forgive him.

Monday she was out of the house before me. It was the last week of school, which meant tests followed by lame parties. Band was done, and I was torn between riding the bus home with Lila and punching in early at the Burger Hut. My mother laughed at me and said, yes, she could drive me over to work when she got home. Walking back from the bus stop, I realized I had been working so much that I rarely saw Foxwood by daylight. The roofs steamed. The ruined chapel sat lumpy under snow. When the three of us reached my stairs, Lily kept walking. In the mailbox, along with a few red-enveloped Christmas cards, was a hand-addressed letter that said only ''Louise.'' It did not have a stamp and was in my father's hand. It was thick. I buried it in the stack and left everything on the counter.

We were nearing the shortest day of the year, and as Lila and I necked on my bed, the bright square of light from my window climbed the wall. *Have you ever been,* Jimi Hendrix asked, *have you ever been to Electric Ladyland?* Lila's hair smelled of strawberry shampoo; we were trading a wad of watermelon bubblegum, making a game of hiding it from the other's tongue. I thought, If I could just stay here.

A little before five we turned the music off and straightened our clothes and smoothed the bedspread and went into the living room to listen for the Country

Squire. My mother came in and said hi to Lila and "Give me five minutes" to me. She riffled through the mail, pausing at my father's letter, then put the stack back on the counter and headed for the bathroom. I kissed Lila goodbye at the door and watched her away.

"You two," my mother commented. "You'd think you were the only people to ever fall in love."

Yes, I wanted to say, in a way we were.

"I'm ready," I said.

On the stairs she asked, "Did your father come by with that letter?"

"I didn't see him."

"You'd tell me if you did."

"Yes," I said defensively.

"Just want to make sure," my mother said.

I worked, totting up my hours like every night at closing. I imagined Lila opening the box and not being able to talk. She would say my name. When Mr. Philbin dropped me off, I looked for the light in her window, but she was asleep. The thought of her warm and peaceful with her glasses off pleased me, made me want to go directly to bed so I could think of her.

My mother was up, watching TV with a drink. She had my father's letter spread across the coffee table. Eight or nine pages of his tiny print. My mother waved a page to show it was both sides.

"Would you look at this?" she said. "Your father has completely flipped his wig."

What does it say? I wanted to ask, but didn't. I figured she would tell me.

"Oh, he's lost it this time. He says he's sorry. Isn't that rich? Sorry!" She shook her head and puffed long on her cigarette. I looked into the kitchen to see if she'd started a new bottle.

She picked up a page and held it close. "Listen to this: 'I see that what I've done to you was unfair.' This is *him* telling *me!* I know this already; what is he telling me for?" She threw the page at the table. "He loves me now. He misses us." She folded her arms and bit her thumbnail. "The fucker!"

She took a drink.

"I'm going to go to bed," I said.

"I'm sorry, Arthur, I don't mean to drag you into this. Go to bed. I'm just angry right now, I'll be fine tomorrow."

"Then I'll see you tomorrow," I said, and she smiled at the joke.

"Okay."

And the next morning she was fine. She went to work, I went to school. Coming home, Lila and I held hands, and Lily sulked. In our mailbox was another letter from my father.

My mother did not show me this one, or quote from it. She had both of them neatly sealed on the coffee table when I came home. She was calm, almost pleasant, and when the news was over, she suggested we both go to bed.

Wednesday she received another, and again Thursday. She did not even open the last one because we were late for her appointment with Dr. Brady. She shoved all four into her purse and we hopped in the car.

"Are you going to be all right with him Saturday?" she asked as we drove along.

"Sure."

"You tell me if you're uncomfortable about it. You can always call me and I'll come pick you up."

"I'll be fine," I said.

"I know," she said. "I know." We went along in silence for a while, past fancy ranches and old mobile homes, until she asked, "Why is he doing this to me?"

I left her at the door of the Hot Dog Shoppe, my wallet heavy with twenties. It was the shortest day of the year; lights dyed the piled snow pink and green. The clerk in Milo Williams knew me by sight. He slid the back of the case open and pulled out the blue velvet box.

"That's the one," I said, and while he gift-

wrapped it I looked at the trays and trays of ugly en-
gagement rings and wedding bands.

My mother was waiting for me in the Hot Dog
Shoppe, polishing off a foot-long with brown mustard.
Her gloves were off, and I noticed her rings, the tiny
diamond and the simple silver band.

"Not much to do today," she explained. "How
much did you drop on Delilah?"

When I told her she winced and shook her head.
"It's your money."

Friday there was another letter, this one thinner.
Bringing it inside, I tried to make out the writing, but
couldn't. Lila suggested we steam it open, which I
didn't find funny. My mother went to her room to
open it, and when she came out later, said nothing.

"She sounds better," Astrid said over the phone.
"What's happening?"

Saturday my father was supposed to pick me up at
five. At a quarter to, we heard his old Nova rumble
up, and then a honk.

"Be nice to him," my mother instructed. "He's
having a hard time. Whatever you do, do not mention
her. You know who I'm talking about."

"Yes," I said.

She did not come to the door.

In the car my father apologized and then was quiet.

He did not offer to let me drive. I had thought I would be able to see the effects of what he had been through in the last week, to read it in his face, but he had not changed at all. He seemed more like my father now than he did when he was with Marcia, and I thought that was good.

"So how have you been?" he asked.

"Okay," I said.

"Talk to your sister lately?"

"Yesterday. She's okay."

"That's good," he said. "What do you say to pizza?"

"Pizza's good."

"Then pizza it is," he said.

We went to the same place he'd taken me our first Saturday. The front window was sprayed with fake frost and dripping with condensation. Monday was Christmas, and we were the only ones there besides the woman behind the counter. My father ordered and we took off our coats. We got our drinks—him a Duke, me a Fanta grape—and picked a table near the window.

We talked at length about the Steelers, and briefly about Annie. He wasn't sure what had happened between her and Glenn Marchand. It was a mystery and a shame. My father said he'd learn more when he went in to work. He'd been out the last couple of days.

I didn't say that I had guessed that.

"So," he said, "I suppose you've heard."

"What?"

"About Marcia."

"Yeah," I said, though it was not really true. No one had told me anything.

"I don't know. I can't explain it to your mother." He picked up the hot-pepper shaker and inspected it. "I fell in love." He put it back down and looked at me again. "It sounds simple, doesn't it?"

"I don't know," I said.

"Nobody believes it. I don't even believe it anymore." He leaned back in his chair and looked up at the ceiling tiles as if stargazing. "That's the funny thing, how it all kind of drains away."

"Large pepperoni!" the woman called, and when he had turned his back to go up and get it, I released a sigh.

"I know it's kind of late to be asking this," he said as we worked on the pie, "but what do you want for Christmas?"

"Tapes are good," I said.

"What else?"

"Oh, I don't know," I said, and came up with four or five things.

We did not talk about him again until he pulled up in front of the coachlight. Instead of letting me out, he turned the car off and followed me up the stairs.

"I need to talk with your mother a second," he explained, the keys still in his hand.

I knocked rather than let myself in, then stood there with him.

My mother opened the door.

"What are you doing here?" she asked my father. She held on to the door, and closed it some after I'd gotten past. My father stood on the landing.

"Did you read my letters?" he asked.

My mother turned her head to see where I was. "Arthur, go to your room. This is private."

I took my time, and then did not close my door all the way. I could see only a sliver of my mother, and beyond her, my father's shoulder. They were talking too softly for me to hear, and then my mother went outside with him and closed the door behind her.

I opened my door and stuck my head out. Nothing.

After a minute I snuck into the kitchen and slowly brought my eyes level with the sill of the front window.

They were standing a few feet apart, my father gesturing with open arms, my mother hugging herself against the cold. My father talked and then waited, bending down to peer into her face.

My mother said one word—"No."

He talked again, palms up, trying to reason with her.

"No," she said, this time loudly enough for me to hear, and followed it with a burst of words. My father stood nodding and looking at the snow between them, and when she was done, turned and headed down the stairs.

I skittered back to my room, just getting the door shut as my mother came inside.

"Arthur?" she called. "He's gone."

I came out and realized I still had my jacket on.

"Did you have a good time?" my mother asked.

"Yeah," I said. "It was okay."

In my room, with the lights out, I thought of Christmases at our old house. I remembered how light the garbage bag full of wrapping paper was; outside we used to throw it around like a boulder, pretending we were Hercules. And the train tracks that gave you a shock if you touched them with your tongue. Needles hid in the carpet; for months you had to wear shoes. In a dish on the mantel the orange my mother had jammed a whole box of cloves into dried and shriveled like a shrunken head. We all had stockings, even my father, who seemed embarrassed that he'd received any gifts. Unluckily, his birthday was December 27. It was a gyp; he ended up getting stiffed. He'd take us all to dinner in Butler, usually Natili's. Once we went to

Pittsburgh, I can't remember where downtown. We had fish.

One New Year's my mother and father went out dancing and left us with Annie. Her father dropped her off in his truck. The minute she was in the door we started following her around. She sat on the floor in the front hall and took her boots off, blew her nose in the bathroom. My mother, in her usual flurry before leaving, went over what snacks we could eat and how late we could stay up, gave Annie the number where they'd be. Annie nodded and smiled; she'd been through this.

"Don't worry," she said. "You're going to be good for me, right, guys?"

We all watched my parents get into the Country Squire and drive away.

"Can we stay up till midnight?" Astrid asked. "Please?"

"When did your mom say you have to be in bed?"

"Ten-thirty," we lied, trying to sound glum.

"Is your mom here?" Annie said.

"No."

"Who's in charge? Who makes the rules?"

"You!" we shrieked, already claiming victory.

"We'll see," she said. "What kind of munchies do you guys want?"

We watched TV, one on either side of her, working at the cheese curls in the bowl on her lap. Astrid brushed her hair, then it was my turn. She let us have Pepsis, as many as we wanted. We jockeyed for her attention, making fun of whatever show was on. Annie turned her wrist over and checked her watch. It was past our bedtime.

"Okay," she said when the bowl was done, "what game should we play?"

"Monopoly!"

"Risk," Astrid voted.

"Arty can't play that yet."

"Life," I tried.

"Life is boring," Astrid said.

"How about Sorry, or Trouble?"

"No," we said.

"Monopoly."

"Okay," Astrid said, "but I get to be banker."

We got down on the floor for it. Annie went upstairs for her cigarettes. As Astrid systematically crushed us with the light blues and purples, I watched Annie smoke, so different from our mother. She wore plum nail polish that she sometimes dabbed on Astrid, but no lipstick. She let a little smoke out of her mouth and made it curl into her nose. She blew a tiny ring through a big one.

"This is no fun, you guys aren't even trying," Astrid said, signaling the end of the game.

"I saw some Klondikes in the freezer," Annie mentioned, as if it were top secret, and we ran upstairs. "First I want you to put your pj's on."

She gave us each a bowl and a spoon and let us take them to the basement, something my mother never did.

Guy Lombardo was on. Times Square was full of people behind long sawhorses marked POLICE. DO NOT CROSS. With five minutes left, Annie made sure everyone had a Pepsi. We counted down, watched the ball drop and then jumped on the couch, screaming. Annie kissed us and we guzzled our bottles like the people on TV, tipping them up and laughing so the bubbles fizzed in our noses.

"All right," she said, "let's get in bed before your mom and dad come back."

"Awww," we protested.

"Get up there."

Astrid was too old for stories. She had her Barbies and a fat Raggedy Ann to keep her company. I waited in bed while Annie tucked her in, listened for the springs to bounce back, then her footsteps.

"It's got to be short tonight," she said in the doorway.

I asked for my favorite, *Charlotte's Web*.

"Too long." She took it from me and sighed, sat

down on the bed and swung her feet up. She smelled of baby powder and cigarettes, with just a hint of their oil burner, and when she reached across me to turn a page I caught a spicy whiff of her herbal deodorant.

She let me keep the book when she was done, pulled the covers up to my chin. I started to ask for another story, but she put a finger to my lips.

"Hush. Go to sleep now."

She started to leave.

"Happy New Year," I said, to make her stay.

She laughed at my inventiveness, came back and leaned over me, her smoky-sweet hair falling like a curtain around my face, and kissed me on the forehead.

"Happy New Year," she said.

Now, in the same bed but in a different house, I wondered why I hadn't missed her before.

The day of Christmas Eve, my mother had to work. It was an easy shift, she said. A lot of the kids went home for the holidays, and she was glad to stay with the ones who were left. They would have a party, and presents; it was not depressing at all. She would be home as early as she could.

I had known all of this in advance, and had invited Lila over for the afternoon. We sat on my bed and talked. I had her present behind the stereo, and when I went to flip the record, I palmed the box. I kissed her and let it drop to the bed behind her. She lay down on it.

"But I didn't bring yours," she argued.

I had to restrain myself from helping her open it.

"Oh," she said, and "Oh," taking it out of the box. "It's beautiful." She held it around her neck. "Put it on me."

I fumbled with the tiny clasp but got it on. She turned and kissed me and we lay down.

We had our shirts off and our jeans unbuttoned when I heard a car slow and stop outside. We both froze and looked toward the front door. A car door closed and someone started up the stairs.

I found Lila's bra and tossed it to her, yanked my shirt over my head, jumped off the bed and closed my door. Lila had her shirt on now; her hair was a mess, as I suspected mine was. I patted my head with both hands and waited for my mother's key in the lock.

The footsteps retreated, going back down the stairs. The car door clunked shut, and the car started.

I ran to the front window in time to see the Nova pull out. Another letter, I thought.

"It's just my father," I called to Lila.

She came out of my room, brushing her hair, then sat down and turned the TV on. The chain looked great.

I put on my shoes and went out to see if he'd left a letter. On the landing sat a huge black garbage bag bursting with presents.

I wrestled it inside.

"Whoa," Lila said. I said that he'd probably done all his shopping in one day. "Whoa," she said again.

My mother said nothing when she saw it. She was late. It was past six and dark and snowing. I had begun to worry. She stopped in the doorway and took off her gloves. She tugged at the bag but it didn't budge.

"Arthur, help me with this."

I came over and got a grip and helped her take it outside.

"Thank you," she said, and motioned for me to go inside. She closed the door behind us, hung up her coat and took off her shoes. "Have you eaten?" she asked, and when I said I was waiting for her, she began making dinner noisily.

She stopped and poured herself a scotch.

"What a perfect day," she said with a sneer, and poured another. "God, I love the holidays."

Later that night, in the middle of *It's a Wonderful*

Life, my father called. My mother was into her ninth or tenth drink and arguing with the TV. She ignored the ringing.

I answered with "Merry Christmas."

"Merry Christmas, Arty," he said.

"Is that him?" my mother asked. "Is that your wonderful father?" She gestured with a finger for me to hand over the phone.

I gave it to her.

"Hey," she said, "just what is the big idea with the fucking Santa Claus bag?"

"You know what I got for you?" she said. "Nothing. Not one goddamn thing. No, no, wait. I got you the divorce. That's your present. So enjoy it. Stick it under your fucking tree and enjoy it."

I headed for my room and put my headphones on. I tried to think of Lila, but all I could see was Annie's girl and then Annie in the water.

I was only on the second song when my mother pushed the door open.

She swayed in the frame. She had been crying and hadn't bothered to wipe her eyes. She came in and sat on the bed, her head bent. She took my hand and held it to her cheek.

"I hope you understand what just happened," she said, "and why it has to be this way."

And I thought that I did and I didn't.

"Arthur."

"I guess," I said, and it was not an evasion. Because though it was already happening to me, I could not see how I would ever come to hate the people I loved. Yet at the same time I could do nothing to stop it, and that would not change for a very long time.

A B O U T   T H E   A U T H O R

STEWART O'NAN received the 1993 Drue Heinz Prize for his short story collection *In the Walled City* and the 1993 Pirate's Alley William Faulkner Prize for his novel *Snow Angels*. He is currently working on a novel about a combat medic in Vietnam, as well as a related screenplay.